Twin Passions

Lora Leigh

ELLORA'S CAVE
ROMANTICA®
ELLORASCAVE.COM

An Ellora's Cave Publication

www.ellorascave.com

Twin Passions

ISBN 9781419967740
ALL RIGHTS RESERVED.
Twin Passions Copyright © 2012 Lora Leigh
Edited by Grace Bradley.
Design by Syneca.
Photography by Shutterstock.com and Fotolia.com

Electronic book publication December 2012
Trade paperback publication 2012

Glossary of Terms

Cauldaran Kings: Lasan and Drago Veraga.

Causeway: A swampy, darkened land that separates part of the magickal lands from the human lands of Yarba.

Consort: A magickal male who has "Joined" with a magickal female.

Consortess: A female of lesser power than a Sorceress who has Joined with a magickal male.

Consortress: A title of distinction given only to Sorceresses who have "Joined" with Wizard Twins.

Coven: A council of twelve who advise the Covenan Queen of royal decisions.

Covenan: The Sorceress lands given to them by The Select when forced to run from the Wizards in fear of their magick and their freedoms.

Covenan Mountain: The greatest center of power in Covenan.

Covenan Sorceress Queen: Amoria Sellane, ruler of the house of Sellane, the ruling family of the Covenani, the sect of the most powerful Sorceresses who separated themselves a millennium before from the Wizard Twins they were aligned with.

Covenan Warriors: Male Sorcerer Warriors who have not yet attained the power of Wizards. Warrior Sentinels. Even the weakest Wizard male is still stronger, much stronger than a sorcerer born of Sorceress and human blood.

Covenani: The Sorceress magick sects.

Covenant of Power: An unnatural joining of Wizards and Sorceress who were not destined to be natural consorts.

Demons: Male humanoid forms of dark magic.

Emerald Valley: Lies within the Royal Mountain Range. Surrounded by towering peaks and mountain walls nearly impossible to scale. A valley all but completely hidden for as long as Covenan has existed. Here, the Griffons are hidden by the Sorceresses.

Garron: The great dragon who helped to raise the Covenani Sorceresses, trained them and now looks over them and their mother. He was assigned by the gods themselves to always protect the ruling Sorceresses of Covenani, especially from the deceptions of the Wizard Twins.

Grandmother Sorceress: The Sorceress who records and holds the history of Sorceress magick.

Griffons: Great flying lions who are so sensitive to dark magick that they know if it is even near, and will attempt to destroy it each time they sense it.

Guardian Keeper of the Lands of the Covenani: Princess Marina, her power and her connection with the land allows her to speak to the others, to hear the lands whisper of evil, of deeds committed.

Guardians of the Cauldaran Lands: Ruine and Raize Veressi.

Guardians of the Power: They oversee and aid the Keepers of the Powers of the Lands (Provinces) and command all the lands.

Guardians of the Power of Sentmar: They hold and protect all the secret pathways of magick, but must be aligned in power and emotion with their natural Consortors/Sentinels Sorceress to be able to use those pathways and to command them at will to protect the land and the people of Sentmar. Once joined with the Sentinel Sorceress, Serena, the Veressi will become the Guardians of Power of Sentmar.

High Sentinel Sorceress Priestess: A Sorceress whose powers are second only to the gods and the Sentinel Sorceress herself. She acts as a bodyguard, companion and friend to the Sentinel Sorceress.

High Sentinel Wizard Priests: One of the most powerful among a select few whose powers are second only to the gods and the Guardian of the Power of Sentmar. They are joined with the High Sentinel Sorceress and act as bodyguards, companions and friends of the Guardian of the Power of Sentmar.

House of Sellane: The ruling family of the Covenani.

Joining: The sexual completion of Wizard Twins and Sorceress mating.

Justice Sorceress: A title bestowed to a Sorceress whose powers can divine or "seer" the truth as well as the level of guilt.

Justice Wizard: A title bestowed to Wizards whose powers can divine the truth as well as the level of guilt.

Keepers of the Lands: Each province has a separate Keeper of the Land. When brought together with the Guardian, they are a powerful fighting and magickal force.

Matriarch Priestess: The highest voice of the coven.

Mystic Forests: One of the four greatest centers of Covenan magick. The forests and mountains hide many beings of great magick.

Natural Consort: The Wizard Twins and Sorceress created to belong to each other. One whose magick and arousal when in the presence of one another rises and amplifies. Wizard Twins accelerate and help balance a Sorceress' power.

Nirvana: The home of the gods.

Pinnacle of Magick: The peak a magickal female experiences once being in contact with her natural Consort. Once brought to life, will not sleep until the peak of alignment has passed, it will then wither and is believed it will not return if a Joining does not occur within the right time frame.

Pixies: Small, delicate females and brawny males. They possess some small magick that's tied directly to the forests they inhabit. They often trade with the magickal beings of Covenan, and only rarely with those of Cauldaran.

Scrye: To be able to see, without the person being present, the answers a magickal being seeks.

Seculars: A human sect determined to destroy the magick of Cauldaran and Covenan and overtake the lands, which are rich in gold, jewels and power, for themselves.

Seer: The ability to see into a being and see the truth or deceit they hold.

Sentinel Select: The gods of Sentmar.

Shadow Hell: Sentmar's underworld.

Shadow Planes: A magickal, often brutal dimension where all forms of magick meet and intertwine. Trials, battles, monstrous forms and dark beings exist there to escape Shadow Hell. Warriors who can "shadow walk" travel through the dark pathways as a shortcut from one part of Sentmar to another. Or they enter there to battle with the dark magick that seeks to step into Cauldaran and Covenan to destroy the beings of magick that live there.

Shadow Walk: The ability to enter the Shadow Planes at will.

Sidhe: They can only be found on a hidden path in the Shadow Planes in the only area known to experience the golden rays of Musera's sun. They are ethereally beautiful, immortal and responsible for bringing humans to Sentmar. They are resented by all of Sentmar's maji for the act and are often called out for it, even now, whenever they are seen. Highly advanced warriors and warrioresses. Whenever traveling outside their own realm they hide within a veil of illusion to ensure they are not identified because they are forbidden to make the first strike when insulted over the act of bringing humans to Sentmar.

Snow Owls: Huge white owls that carry Wizard and Warrior Twins into battle.

Sorcerer: Of human and Sorceress or Wizard's blood. In essence, a magickal Halfling of much lesser or no magickal abilities at all (not of Wizard and Sorceress birth).

Sorceress: The highest feminine powers. They were meant to battle next to their Twins, and to provide a base of power for their Twins to tap into.

Sorceress Brigade: A unit of two dozen Sorceress "Keeper" initiates (daughters of Keepers of the Lands) also known as the Sorceresses in waiting to the Queen or the Princesses.

Sorceress Justice: A group of sorceresses charged with deciding the guilt and innocence of those suspected of criminal acts.

Sorceress Keepers of the Land: Twelve Keepers of the Power of the lands (provinces) of Covenan.

Sorceress Priest: The second most powerful female on the planet.

Sorceress Sentinel of Power: The highest reigning female of magick who legend says will appear during times of war or danger to Covenani or the ruling house of Sellane.

The One: The highest of all Sentmar power worshipped by the magickal beings as the Sorcerer Select and by the humans.

The Reigning Age: The age when Keeper heirs normally return to their lands to take their throne and begin ruling the power of their province.

The Vale of Sorcery: Exists within the Shadow Planes. The place where dark magick rules and Wizard Twins battle against the creatures dark magick attempts to send through the pathways to the magickal lands.

Unicorns: Pure white horses with golden horns that are tied exclusively to the Sorceresses of Covenan. They will rarely allow males of any sect to ride them. Some unicorns bond with their riders to such an extent that they can communicate with them psychically.

Unit Select: One Sorceress is created to complete each set of Wizard Twins. To bind the Sorceress and the Twins in a ring of magickal pleasure and power.

Witches and Warlocks: Having more power than a magickal human, but less than a Sorcerer or Sorceress. Witches and Warlocks are mostly working class.

Veressi line: Guardians of the Land of Cauldaran for as long as there have been record of such things. Just as the house of Sellane had birthed the Guardian of Covenan since they had claimed Covenan as their own. Their rage and petty deceptions had been the cause of countless Sorceress deaths in those first years after the separation between the two magicks.

Winter Mountains: So bitterly cold only magickal beings can survive there, though none are known to exist there.

Wizard: The third most powerful males on the planet.

Wizard Priests: The second most powerful males on the planet.

Wizard Sentinel: The most powerful and revered of the ancient Wizards.

Wizard Twins: Twins born with such an elemental bond that it is more comfortable and their power more powerful when they Join with the same Sorceress. They always complement each other. One may be impatient, the other patient. One determined, the other easygoing. One Wizard always counters or balances each other. Wizards do not make deals or pacts without their Twins' knowledge of it.

Wizard Moons: The two "male" moons of Sentmar. Once three thick rings of magick surrounded them as they moved across the sky, said to always be searching for their one true Sorceress, the sun. For a millennium they've been growing transparent and wispy as the power of the land seems to be growing weaker.

Yarba: The human province that borders the Causeway.

Once, Sentmar had no humans.

It was a place of beauty, of magick, of innocence.

Power whispered and lingered like wisps of morning moisture upon the air. It glistened and sparkled like fortune's gems and trilled its sweet magick like the song of the tweeterlings.

Then, the Sidhe brought to Sentmar humans from a realm where violence and fear subverted magick.

These humans, they swore, understood all magicks. They swore they were creatures of peace who only sought to escape the death that followed them for their loyalty to the Sidhe.

Our councils protested this addition. Our Seers saw a darkness on the horizon arriving with these creatures. Our rulers listened to the sad tale of these humans with trepidation. And we denied the Sidhe their request. We wanted not the humans they sought refuge for, though we knew great sympathy for their plight.

The Sidhe, being the Sidhe, listened to naught but their own wants. They brought these humans and placed them in the one place they knew we would not sense the darkness in their souls.

At least, not for a while.

By the time we found these creatures they had multiplied. Like nothing we had known on Sentmar, they rooted themselves to the land the Sidhe had placed them on and called it their own. A land that had once thrived with the fragile buds of magick spreading into it. A land whose magick became hidden, frightened and cowering in the shadows like the children those humans would strike at their whims.

The Sidhe refused to remove them. They refused to aid us in transferring them back to their own realm. We, the magickal beings, the children of Sentmar, were in danger of extinction.

We were the many, they were the few.

We were the strong, they were the weak.

Yet we could not will them to leave, and our laws forbade drenching the land in their blood.

And what we feared came to pass.

The humans soon began spreading even into lands that magick had held from the beginning of our creation. Each step they took upon Sentmar, soon, magick would ease away. It would hide. It would watch in fear, uncertain and frightened as the dark hearts of these beings began to look toward even the lands of the greatest power.

Lands fed by the Raging Seas of Magick, a monstrous body of water that fills half this wondrous land. The waters of mystery, strength and power where creatures of wonder, of brilliance and power lurk within its liquid magick and watch as they feed into the streams, the channels and the lakes that build and run beneath the very lands themselves.

Or they once did.

We begged the Sidhe to remove their wards.

They refused.

We pleaded with them.

They turned a deaf ear.

And the humans moved over Sentmar like a plague as magick slid slowly to the shadows, even within Cauldaran.

Our Seers became weak.

Wizards were being birthed as one rather than as twins. Sorceresses were being condemned for their power, and in terror we watched as our magick began to hide even within us.

The feel of magick strangling within the lands awakened our creator, the father of all magick. The One.

Traveling across Sentmar he saw the invasion, the fear, the cruelties of humans and the dimming of the glory of the sun that warmed the skies and heated the magick that ran in vast pools and molten streams beneath the lands.

It was being destroyed by creatures whose darkness could not be denied. Even they, try as they might, and try often, could not deny it themselves.

On the throne of Cauldaran at this time sat a princess, ruling alone. One whose magick was great and as pure as her flesh who had never known a lover's touch. Serving as her most trusted guards were one of the few sets of Wizard Twins who still yet existed. Wizards whose power was as pure as their princess's innocence and fed by the Raging Seas themselves.

To these Wizards and to this princess Sorceress he came in a dream. He showed them magick like none had ever known. He showed them the hidden moon within the skies behind its brother. He showed them the power of the twin moons as both became revealed. The thick, luminous rings that would surround them, that would wrap around the sun as well and add to the power of the magick of the land. And they would be the first to know this wondrous gift.

On the night the twin moon forced itself from hiding and the rings of magick began to surround both, the Wizard Twin protectors and Sorceress princess would Join and their magick would build. They would Join, and they would pull Wizard Twins from hiding and magickal Sorceresses from the shadows.

In their Joining, magick would build once again. That magick would give his children the power to push back the darkness that had come to Sentmar with the arrival of the humans.

As the One promised, the day came that the twin moon moved out of hiding and its thick, pillowy clouds surrounded both moons and the sun as well. That day, Wizard Twin Consortors took as their Consortress the princess Sorceress.

The Raging Seas began to whip as though in fury. Great waves pounded at the shores, flooded the human towns that had grown upon them and forced the pestilence back to the lands from whence the Sidhe had bid them stay.

Magick invaded the streams, the lakes. It boiled and burned and spewed from volcanoes in far-off lands. Spores of magick began to fill the air, infused the soil, the lakes and streams, the creatures of four legs and the creatures of two and all the creatures the One had meant for it to fill.

Humans were the invaders. They were alien to the land and to the magick, and they were driven back. Magick seared their senses, caused great bolls of darkness to rise beneath their flesh and turned their eyes a bloody hue, marking them as a creature unwanted by the magick lands.

The rules the One had given all of magick, he was forced to abide as well. He could not shed the blood of the humans and wipe them from the planet. He could not take from the lands he had created what the Sidhe had brought to it. He could banish the darkness-diseased forms instead.

He could push them back to the lands they were given by creatures who had no rights to bequeath it. Between that land and the rest of Sentmar, great mountains rose. A dark, putrid channel formed at the base of the great mountains, so wide, so deep, that even to magick it appeared daunting and fearsome.

Creatures of vengeful magick were placed there. Creatures whose hatred of humans consumed them, rose from the muck, the mire and the pools of bubbling magick. The air in this place of disease and death was commanded to burn and to sear those who lacked magick.

The creatures the darkness of that place gave birth to were filled with but one purpose. To hold back the dark death called "human". These creatures alone were given leave to spill the blood on the interlopers, whether crime was committed or not. Whether first blood was drawn or not.

No matter the reason, the why or the excuse. Should humans attempt to cross the causeway the One had created, then their lives would be forfeit.

Turned he then to the Wizards and Sorceresses he had gifted. He bade them, hear him well. As long as Wizards and Sorceress came together by natural magickal selection, so then would they always grow in power.

As long as Wizards knew gentleness, as long as they knew love. As long as Wizards aligned with their natural Consortress, so then would they always know peace.

Should Wizards force their Sorceresses to unions of power, rather than love, they would know regret. Should Wizards steal a Sorceress' will, steal her strength, her freedom and her magick, so then would they lose the gifts the One had bequeathed them.

Should Wizards ever, at any time, force a Sorceress to turn from her natural Consorts to a union of power, while taking to their bed the Sorceress who should have been their own, so then would he take from them the one gift that would surely weaken them forever.

He would take from them their Sorceress.

Then, from the Winter Mountains, at the very boundary of Cauldaran, he drew the great Snow Owls where they hunted and nested. Those great feathered beasts emerged from within a wintery landscape of such chill that even magickal beings were known to find death's arms awaiting their journeys into them.

The pure white owls, fierce and strong, would carry the Wizards high above the lands to ensure humans never invaded again. They would protect and transport their Wizards and give to them their fierce loyalty and devotion.

From the frozen, ice-filled vales of those mountains and the valley beyond where spring always bloomed, the One then drew the great winged lions to forever serve the Sorceresses who may one day have only the strength of the fierce beasts to save them.

Each gift was strong, sure, fierce in battle and determined in loyalty. Each placed their fates in the hands of those the One sent them to serve and to protect. To watch over these children the One so adored and forever see to their survival.

For a time, magick reigned. Wizard Twins and Sorceresses of love, beauty and magickal centers so pure and strong they infused the air around them, united as the One commanded.

Until Twin kings looked at the daughter who would rule and knew regret. A daughter who refused the Wizard Twins brought to her, who searched desperately for Consorts who seemed forever distant. She would take the throne, she would rule as one rather than as one of three. And this they could not abide.

To Wizards of power he sought a bargain. His daughter and her throne in exchange for a Joining of power rather than of love.

It was a bargain they eagerly accepted. One they were grateful to be given, for the Sorceress destined to be theirs had been lost to them forever by another such bargain but a short time before.

Wizards were trading their daughters to unions of power rather than love. Parents were promising their newly born Sorceresses to boy Wizards while their parents profited.

All the One had said was forbidden was now practiced often. And after a time, it soon became rare for natural Joinings to find approval. From there, it was not but a step to a law that made illegal any Joining not approved by the Wizard Chancellors to each province of Cauldaran.

And soon, all too soon, Wizard Rulers took as Consortress a Sorceress who longed for her natural Consorts. Outside that Joining they took the Sorceress their hearts longed for, and denied her forevermore their magick souls they had aligned with another.

What had once been ecstasy, a pleasure so incredible that only those of magick could bear its sweet bite, became agony instead. One Sorceress taken by Twins who knew no love, no tenderness. Twins whose magick knew only regret and resentful greed.

And it was the Sorceresses who paid the price. With their pain, their fear. With their hearts and their compassion. They paid for the greed of Consorts, power-hungry fathers, mothers, sisters, aunts and cousins filled with cold misery and loss and unable to bear the sight of another Sorceress finding that which brought the greatest pleasure.

Until those of the first Joining, that princess Sorceress and her Twin protectors whom the One gave rule to Nirvana once their lives upon Sentmar expired, heard the wails and felt the tears of their magickal descendants below.

The twin moons, it is written by some, knew compassion and aided their Consortress in leading their daughters from

Cauldaran to a land some said only the Griffons knew the way to.

Others have written that the goddess looked down upon hearing a single heartbeat expire. A Sorceress of her direct line, taken, imprisoned within a cold and lonely castle, the mistress of Twins who had aligned for power rather than taking the Sorceress their magick reached out for. A Sorceress who could no longer bear the pain, both of body and of spirit. The first Sorceress ever recorded to have committed the ultimate sin and taken her own life.

Musera, the Sorceress the One chose as goddess to his lands, it is written by some, aided the Sorceresses' bid for freedom and sent to them the knowledge of the lands filled with magick that lay across the great frozen expanses of Winter Mountains and the Feral Glaciers that lay beyond.

Those same historians wrote that when the Twin gods saw what their goddess had taken from their sons, that rage struck all of Sentmar. They wrote that on that day, Wizard Twins and Sorceress Consortresses battled with the same fierce fury and determination as the Twin gods and their goddess fought above.

Anger, pain and rebellion surged through the lands, it was written, no matter the historian writing it.

The Raging Seas swept upon the shores and pounded at the base of the mountains. Blinding magickal snows and ice pelted Winter Mountains while volcanoes opened upon their snowy peaks and shed their molten magick, melting ice and snow as they fell to the mountains below.

The historians wrote the event as the day Cauldaran lost warmth. The day the magick set back in shock and pain and watched as the heart of Cauldaran was torn asunder.

And both wrote the Keepers of the Power of Cauldaran, those entrusted with the heart of magick, the secrets, the power, the very spirit of magick, used it to strike against the most tender, and yet the most fierce of the children of that land.

The daughters of the One.

Sorceresses and Twins battled as the great flying lions, the Griffons of Sentmar, fought to protect the Sorceresses given to their keeping. Blocking the paths, roaring out their rage as the magickal Twins struck them down and filled the base of the mountains with the Griffons' blood.

What they did not kill, they enchanted. The females and babes were blocked from their inner magick then sent to the dark, violent realms of the Shadow Planes. A place so infected with the darkness of evil that survival was highly unlikely.

For centuries rage filled Cauldaran.

Wizards warred for lands, for power, for the few Sorceresses of lesser magick and the magickal descendants of human Joinings whose power was minimal, yet still, 'twas power to access.

The Raging Seas boiled with the fury of the gods. Storms swept the land, fought to cross the Winter Mountains yet rarely crossed to the Valley of Spring beyond.

For a hundred years Wizard Twins existed in a haze of blood-red rage. Until the descendants of those first Keepers crossed the great icy barrier and kidnapped the Sorceress the magick of that newly discovered magickal land had claimed.

A Keeper of the Power is bonded with the land and the magick it holds. In Cauldaran, she built the power of the land she oversaw, fighting to strengthen it, to hold back the weakness that unnatural Joinings had brought to it.

In Covenan, a Keeper controlled the magick of a center of power that boiled and surged, burned and raged beneath the land like an ungoverned child. Her magick centers it, soothes it and gives it purpose.

On that day, the Keepers of Cauldaran magick, Twins who harness the power of the Raging Seas, slipped into the lands the Sorceresses hid within and stole the Keeper the lands had just chosen.

Once forcing an alignment and taking the Sorceress their magick longed for, they cruelly and without thought tore from her soul the bonds the land had made with her.

Suddenly bereft, a piece of her heart, a portion of her soul missing, the Sorceress wept and grieved until her young heart could take no more. Leaping from the tallest tower of the castle she was imprisoned within, the Keeper of the Power of the Royal Forests of Covenan threw herself to her death.

The magick of Covenan grieved.

The magick of Cauldaran threatened to tear the lands apart with its rage.

If the gods were in opposition over the separation of Wizard Twins and Sorceress Consorts, then in their horror and disbelief at the actions of the magickal Twins they were united.

A surge of power swept over the lands of both magickal sects. Musera closed the remaining portals between Cauldaran and Covenan. Her Twin Consorts blocked their sons' magick from ever breaching the divide from Cauldaran again. And together, the three ensured no Sorceress could ever be taken by force from her lands again.

The wound created that day was one the gods feared would never heal within their daughters. They watched as the centuries passed. As the divide between the magicks continued to grow.

They watched as the magick of all of Sentmar began to weaken.

The great billowy clouds of magick surrounding the twin moons began to dim. Humans began to strike and something dark and malevolent began to fill the land.

The One awoke once again, looked out at the danger to the daughters he so loved, and knew he must act once more.

The darkness that lurked in Shadow Hell could only be held back by the magick of Wizard Twin and Sorceress unions. Joinings natural to the hearts and souls of those unions, rather than the forced alignments his daughters had once suffered.

A millennium passed, and still, Wizard Twins had not seen past their arrogance and the mistakes of the past. If he did not act, if he did act quickly, then all of magick would be destroyed and the humans would persecute his children until nothing remained of them.

But he must be careful.

He must be diligent.

The darkness was strong, the magick was weak, and still his children knew a division that threatened all of the lands of magick.

That threatened their very existence.

Prologue

"It is the Keeper of the Power of Covenan that we are here to Court, Rhydan, we must not forget this," Torran Delmari stated, his voice so dark and filled with sensual warmth it lit a fire inside Astra Al'madere that she could not cool, nor eradicate. "No matter our desires otherwise, she must be found."

She opened her eyes slowly and watched the warriors as they stood now, their backs to her, their voices lowered.

Trembling, shaking with such pain and betrayal she distantly wondered why her magick wasn't filling the hall with the furious sparks of her rage, she fought to hold back her tears.

Her outrage.

She could feel it crackling inside her, threatening to spark from her body and strike about the gracious Covenani marble columns and striking sparkspur stone floors that gleamed with hues of darkened red before blending into lush, red-orange streaks of the magick stone. Covenani marble and sparkspur tone amplified female power, called to it, and would have surely betrayed her had she not learned at an early age to contain her pain.

She was going to die from the effort though.

She was certain of it.

Deep in her heart, in her soul, where her magick protected her even against her tender Sorceress emotions, Astra could feel herself weakening, losing the will to stand to her feet, to protect herself from falling into the yawning pit of agony that opened inside her fragile spirit.

Her eyes filled with moisture, tears that were all but unheard of for the heir to the Keeper of the Mystic Forests.

Astra Al'madere did not cry.

Were these Wizards not aware of the laws of magickal Joinings?

Fools.

They were such fools.

Of course they were aware.

The magick that existed inside all magickal beings that was responsible for finding their natural Consort would not tolerate such betrayal of the natural ways of courtship.

Did they not remember why Wizards and Sorceresses separated a millennium before? How could they not know that once they sought to betray their natural Consort, their magick would forever hide her identity from them until the day they rectified that most heinous mistake?

She had not shed tears since those first nights after her mother, the Keeper of the Mystic Forests, had sent her from her land and gave her to the keeping of the Queen of Covenan.

She had thought, believed with all her soul, that no betrayal could ever be greater than the betrayal of a beloved mother.

As the golden rays of the life-giving sun spilled their heated magick into the receiving hall, Astra learned there were far greater betrayals.

There was the betrayal of a Sorceress' Wizard Twins. Her Consorts, and the Wizards she alone had been created for.

She slowly flattened her back against the great stone column of the entry hall of the castle Sellane, the ruling house of the land of Covenan.

She could not believe what she heard. Surely she must have misunderstood.

Turning slowly, silently, she peeked around the column to where the two great warriors stood, discussing matters they would have done well to discuss in private.

Torran's eyes, a deeper blue than even that of the Raging Magick Seas, like Rhydan's lighter blue ones, were narrowed and glittering with irritation. Shielded by the enviously long black lashes that surrounded them, they gleamed the color of pure magick. Hair as black as the deepest night fell about their wide shoulders and emphasized the white of their cord cotton shirt, while their black warriors pants outlined their lean, powerful hips.

The crystalline spores of power, invisible but intuitive, reached out from the Wizard Twins, always seeking, always on alert for even the most hidden sign of danger.

It was a magick she did not fear though, one that whispered over her as it had before, caressing her with an invisible touch of such exquisite pleasure that she could only close her eyes weakly and acquiesce to it rather than protest.

Protesting would mean allowing them to know she was there. For some reason, their magick never alerted them to her presence.

The magick that filled the two men was so strong though. So strong that their natural Consortress felt it reaching out desperately for her, twining around her with a hint of confusion.

How very odd, she thought as her neck arched to the heated warmth that stroked over it, caressing the sensitive flesh with a slow, delicious touch of magick. She could sense the strength of the intuitive magick these warriors possessed as it sought her out, confused why she did not reveal herself to the Wizards standing just beyond the column.

The urge to go to them, to reveal herself and her knowledge that they were her natural Consorts was an impulse so very difficult to deny. An impulse that only grew at the knowledge that *her* Consorts were seeking another.

"Did you hear me, brother?" the eldest Delmari Wizard questioned harshly.

"I have not gone deaf, Torran. I but question this plan you intend to enact. I am not so certain it is the wisest course to take," Rhydan snapped. "Already I feel our Consortress, I feel our magick reach for her and I am certain we met her the day of our arrival. As much as I agree with the Veressi in their present plan, still, this reeks of a deception I am not certain needs to be practiced." As he spoke, their magick feathered against the lobe of her ear, the ghostly tug of its touch urged her once again to reveal herself.

"And for that reason alone I am most grateful that it was not of my design. Should you suspect who our Consortress is, then I beg of you, brother, do not reveal such to me." Torran sighed. "I can do naught but pray to the Select that we are doing what is best for all concerned and that soon this will be over."

What plan? If only they had entered the great hall sooner, perhaps when they were discussing the details of it rather than arguing the advisability of it, then Astra would at least have information to give to the Guardian of the Power of the Lands of Covenan and the commander of the Sorceress Brigade.

"We are to attempt to convince her to align with us in a Covenant as our Consortress and we are not even certain which Sorceress she is." Torran seemed to be reminding him. "The Guardian of the Lands of Covenan hides herself well, but she is the only Consortress the Veressi will accept for us if we wish to ensure our lands remain within Delmari control as it has since the dawn of Wizard magick."

Agony struck at her once more. She could not believe they would do this. Since their arrival mere days before she had known who they were to her. And she knew now, they sensed her. They might not know which Sorceress she was, but they sensed her. She had known she was their Consortress, yet they would take another instead? They would force the alignment of magicks rather than coming to her, the Sorceress who had

24

awaited them since she had awakened to her female power and desires? They searched for another as Consortress, when they knew, she knew, they must be aware that their Consortress was near.

How had this happened? What stroke of insanity would make them consider such an act? To convince a Sorceress to "align" with them? Such an unnatural act of Consortship would never be considered by any Sorceress, especially the one Astra knew as the Guardian of Covenan.

"What of the one our magick seeks? Even now I feel it reaching out to her," Rhydan asked then, his voice heavy. "I still cannot learn which Sorceress it is, as though the weave of magick that has searched evermore for her now refuses her identity to us. It is now to the point I believe I fear the ball to introduce the Sorceresses to those of us who have come seeking Consortresses."

"Perhaps it is better we do not know which Sorceress it is, brother." Torran sighed regretfully. "To know, yet to be unable to touch, unable to take her as our own, surely would be a fate worse even than seeking a Consortress not our own to possess."

She could not bear this pain.

She could not bear such a betrayal.

Remaining hidden, feeling the consoling caress of their magick and the regret that lay heavy within it, Astra could only bite back the furious anger growing inside her, even as a single tear escaped her control.

A second later she felt their magick receding as they walked away and took with them the pleasure spilling over her body.

Her fists clenched as she felt her breathing accelerate, felt the searing betrayal burning with such white-hot force it weakened her will to hold back the fury rising in answer.

What manner of evil could possess warriors, Wizard Twins, to deliberately turn their backs on their natural

Consortress for a Consortress whose Twins were already set to claim her? Wizards more than willing to kill to claim the Sorceress these two sought.

And well they would deserve such death, she thought furiously.

Wizard Twins were once known to kill over the Sorceress they claimed not just with their magick but with their hearts as well. And no doubt, the Sashtain Twins would kill for Marina.

The thought of the deaths of the Delmari Twins filled her with dread though. Could she survive if such happened? She feared she wouldn't. But she was also aware that the Sashtain Twins would only kill should another actually try to take Marina from their hold, something Rhydan and Torran would never accomplish.

But the betrayal was destructive to her heart.

It ate at her.

The pain bloomed inside her until once again one lone tear fell. And with that tear came another. The proof of a broken heart spilling from her like beads of moisture from the Weeping Trees whose crystalline drops were said to bring comfort from the Sorceress Select herself.

There was no comfort to be found for Astra from her own tears. There was nothing to ease her pain, nothing to still the aching sorrow in her soul.

There was only the knowledge that her warriors had no desire to be her Consorts.

First betrayed by a mother who refused to love, and now by the Consorts who turned their backs on her as well.

She was as she had always hoped she would not be.

Alone.

Chapter One

ঔ

Magic.

It whispered through the castle.

Heavy tendrils of invisible power moved along the castle halls, slid around the corners, eased its way beneath locked doors and eavesdropped amid Wizard Twins.

Thankfully, the eavesdropping part wasn't her job, Astra thought morosely as she stood guard at the entrance to Princess Marina's wing of the castle. She had had enough of the inner thoughts of Wizard Twins each time she had drawn near to the Wizards who should have been her own.

Who should have been her own...

Holding back her grief was a near impossible task, and yet one she knew she must persevere to succeed at. Because failure would mean revelation. It would mean revealing herself as the natural Consortress to those who were now sought as criminals. As practitioners of the dark arts. As murderers.

She stared straight ahead along the hall, pushing back the agony, the sorrow. Pushing back a pain unlike anything she could have imagined existing.

She had believed nothing could be worse than knowing her Consorts and being unable to reveal herself to them. She had believed nothing could be worse than knowing Wizard Twins who should have been her own sought another as their Consortress.

There was a greater pain.

There was the pain of knowing those her heart and Sorceress spirit was already tied to were now known as the most vile of any in the land. To add to that pain was the knowledge that shed her tears. To release the grief, that now only built within her soul, would be to reveal herself. And should she do such, then she could be used to draw those dark Wizards from wherever they hid and force them to be brought to justice.

Could she live with the knowledge that their first glimpse of her as their Consortress would also be as the one who had betrayed them?

She could not bear such knowledge.

She could not bear allowing such to happen.

Standing guard, she and another warrioress of the Princess Brigade reinforced the magick of the Guardian of the Power of Covenan. They stood ready should any enemy manage to get past both the magickal guards the Sashtain Twins had set in place as well as the protective power of the land that the Guardian of the Power of Covenan commanded.

She carried on each hour, knowing each second, each minute, could be the last that she could hold back this pain.

Not that she or the others could do much if anyone or anything managed to slip past such vast power.

As the tendrils of magick wove across the land, Astra could feel the faintest disturbance reaching out to her, calling for her.

The demand was faint, weak, though not in peril. There was no danger, yet the demand was one she couldn't ignore either. It pulled at her. It poked at her like a child determined to be heard.

Shifting restlessly, she glanced around the hall, uncomfortable with ignoring the demand, yet not entirely certain from where it came. Closing her eyes, she allowed her senses to open further, to expand and reach out to the call. It could be a Sorceress in need. Although they did not face peril at this moment, it did not mean they would not face it soon. As her answering magick touched the call once more, she sensed, rather than Sorceress or other female magickal being, it was instead an animal in need.

She never knew which creatures, with or without magick, would reach out to her, or even if they would. The affinity she seemed to have with the creatures of Covenan drew her often from her duties at the castle. Until now, that hadn't been a problem.

But with Queen Amoria and her heir Serena having been stolen from the castle, and all Sorceresses on high alert and determined that their last remaining princess, the Guardian of the Power of Covenan, not be taken from them as well, Astra fought to ignore the summons.

There was no true peril.

Frowning, she attempted to identify the call, but either it was too immature or too weak to identify itself.

Whichever, she knew that ignoring it would not be an option soon.

"I can sense the disturbance as well," the Sorceress standing guard with her, Aerin, Keeper heir of the Whispering Mountains said quietly. "You cannot ignore it."

"I cannot leave." Astra sighed in regret. "Should our Guardian have need of me…"

The other Sorceress gave a slow shake of her head and a gentle smile. "Even I hear the call the land is sending out to you, Keeper." She smiled back, though the somber concern in her gaze belied any amusement or joy. "Go, heed its summons, I will call another to stand guard over the Guardian's quarters with me."

The land was indeed calling out to her, not just the creature in need. This was a demand that even the land itself felt important. A strident summons, one without blood, but one of imperative determination that she heed the demand reaching out to her magick with such fierce voracity.

"Think you need a Sorceress to accompany you?" Aerin asked, her gentle violet eyes watching Astra closely. "Perhaps Camry has rested enough to ride along."

Astra gave a sharp shake of her head. "There is no danger. Perhaps one of the Unicorns in need." She frowned. "The call is one of an animal spirit, though nothing in dire danger."

"So I felt as well," Aerin agreed. "I'll call Camry to stand with me and we will watch over Serena as you do what you must."

Astra feared the summons was more than a simple animal in need though. The call came from the Emerald Valley, the site of the battle that had raged between the Guardian Keeper of the lands, Marina, and the dark magick that had attempted to take the valley where the Griffons' lair was located.

Her chest clenched at the thought of the Griffons as she all but ran through the tunnels to reach the cavern where several Unicorns awaited the Sorceresses' needs for transportation.

The new stable caretaker, Azeron, an old and wizened fellow of undetermined age, was securing the light leather saddle the Sorceresses used on the stallion Tripelli as she entered the room.

As she reached the beast he slid the leather halter over its head and handed her the reins.

"The Eastern passage into the Emerald Valley has been cleared." He spoke softly, his voice roughened with age. "I arrived from that direction and saw the Unicorn foals at play. The way is shorter."

"You knew my direction how?" She frowned at him as she vaulted into the saddle.

A chuckle rasped from his throat. "You told this fair beast." He patted the stallion's neck as it pawed the ground impatiently. "It was he who told me."

The new caretaker's accord with the Unicorns had been the only reason the Guardian of the Lands and Princess Serena had allowed him the privilege of caring for the Unicorns that rested within the cavern stables.

The Unicorns seemed to cherish him. Often nuzzling at him for affection, despite the fact he rarely brought them treats. They simply enjoyed his touch.

Giving a sharp nod, she leaned over the stallion's neck and without command, Tripelli rose to his back legs, pawed the air then came down with a jump that had him shooting from the cavern and making the sharp turn that led to the narrow eastern passage to the Emerald Valley.

Rains often swelled the stream that ran through the passage to dangerous levels, making it hazardous for the Unicorns to cross at the two points where no other path could be taken. If it were clear, then it would remain so until the next hard rains, and would cut the journey to the Emerald Valley by more than half the distance.

Tripelli charged through the Royal Forest, heading for the eastern entrance to Emerald Valley. Powerful legs and a wide chest ensured his endurance, and with the wind playing haphazardly through his mane and Astra's curls, it was as close as the Sorceresses came to flying until the Griffons had been found.

The eastern passage was wide, filled with lush green grass and sheltering trees. As the caretaker said, the Unicorn mares and their foals frolicked in the small vale and splashed about the stream that wound through it.

The closer she came to the Emerald Valley, the more painful the thought of returning there became.

The spell that had turned the Griffons to stone had been reversed, but for two. The infant male, Tambor, and the half-grown male, Candalar, who had been broken cruelly while in stone form.

Their healers had no idea how to repair the damage, or if repair were even possible. Arrangements would be made to bring them to the castle. Until then, they had been left as they lay, Marina's fears that even the smallest shard of stone could be lost in the transfer making the decision for her.

Yet, surprisingly she could now sense both males, where before she had not, as she neared the area where they had been left.

Weak. The magick that flowed through them was barely existent, though it had been nonexistent before.

Where once she had felt nothing when she searched for their location, she now felt their warmth, Tambor's confusion, though not his fear. Candalar was irritated, though neither appeared in distress.

Or if they were, they were unaware of it.

But they wanted her with them now.

She had played with them for many years, soothed their minor wounds caused by play, and often teased them for their clumsiness.

She was one of their favored caretakers, and the closer she came to the area where they had been left broken and discarded, the louder their summons seemed to grow.

Her ears were ringing with the roars they now sent along the telepathic pathways. Her head was buzzing with their demands that she come to them.

Urging Tripelli to greater speed, she held tight to the heavy mane, her gaze narrowed against the wind and her own thoughts.

How could they be calling out to her? How much more heartache could she bear than to hold the cold stone to her breast and know she could not return them from the cold stone forms they had been turned into? There could be no evil greater than that which the Justice Layel had practiced upon the innocent Griffon babes. And no horror Astra imagined could be greater to the cubs.

32

May the Sentinel Select protect any other being with the slightest thought to harm more of those creatures.

Marina might believe others were more powerful than Astra. She might be uncertain where Astra's powers were concerned. But Astra was not uncertain. Neither was she unprepared to spill blood in the defense of the animals she had grown so fond of.

Animals that were stone, their magick silenced since the moment the Justice Layel had touched the perverted spell upon them, was surely an evil punishable by the fiery horrors of Shadow Hell.

Clearing the stream and entering the valley, Tripelli took his own path, following his connection with Astra to find his way to the emanations of magick that called to her.

Winding through the edges of the Emerald Valley, sheltered by the heavily leafed, sheltering trees of the Royal Forest, Astra could feel the hope beginning to burn inside her that somehow the spell had been reversed and the cubs were calling out for soothing strokes along their backs or the warm baths the Sorceresses provided.

Surely she would not find cold stone.

Surely it was not the still, gray forms she would find as the cubs' spirits cried out to her.

The horror of that thought tore at her chest and filled her eyes with tears as the Unicorn made a wide turn around the huge boulders that rested on the forest floor as though tossed there by the gods' restless play.

Rounding the great stone spheres, the Unicorn came to a sliding stop, his rump nearly touching the ground at the sight that lay across his path.

A sob tore from her lips, a gasping cry of shock at what she found and her inability to process such a sight.

It could not be.

The Delmari Twins. The Wizard traitors both Covenan Warrioresses and Cauldaran Wizard and Sorcerer Warriors were searching for to question in regard to dabbling in dark magick and leading that perverted power into the Griffons' lair. The two warriors Astra had fought to forget, to push from her soul at the knowledge that they had disappeared before the battle in the valley for the Griffons had ended.

It was believed they had fled from the fight, refusing to battle against the dark evil because they called it master. They were accused of betraying both Sorceresses and Wizards to the dark magick, without care of the consequences.

But it wasn't dark magick she saw as she slid from the Unicorn's back and approached cautiously. It was not evil that the land and the Griffon cubs were whispering to her, rather a demand for aid.

Lying beside the Wizard Twins' unconscious forms were the fully intact, living, breathing, if weakened, forms of the Griffon babes she believed she would never see romping about the valley again.

What caused her to do what she did next, she couldn't explain.

Well she could, but it was an explanation she didn't want to venture into at the moment. It was one she couldn't allow herself to venture into.

Instead, she joined her Wizards in treason.

Chapter Two

The battle for the land of the Sorceresses was one that drained all who fought it.

The magick of the Covenan Sorceress Brigade, twelve warrior Sorceresses — led by the Guardian of the Lands of Covenan, the Guardian of all feminine magick, and commanded by the heir in waiting of the Covenan throne — had nearly lost all they held dear in the battle.

They had been betrayed by one of their most revered Justices, a Sorceress charged with deciding the guilt and innocence of those suspected of criminal acts. And she herself had committed one of the most heinous crimes known. She had betrayed her own to the dark arts and a shadowed evil that had nearly destroyed Emerald Valley.

Lying within the Royal Mountain range, surrounded by towering peaks and nearly unscalable mountain walls, the Emerald Valley had been all but hidden for as long as Covenan had existed.

And here, the Sorceresses had hidden one of their greatest treasures, the nearly extinct flying lions. Creatures whose love and loyalty to the Sorceresses they had been gifted to had been betrayed once before by Cauldaran warriors, and now betrayed again by the Justice who had led that dark evil to them in this once secured valley.

The Griffons' loyalty and bond to the Sorceresses had nearly destroyed them a millennium ago when they had fought to protect the fleeing Consorts of the Cauldaran Wizards.

The Guardians and Keepers of the Cauldaran lands had wiped their inherent memories and instincts from them, leaving them undefended and without the knowledge of the strength and power they possessed to protect themselves. They had then been sent to the dark desolation of the Shadow Planes, a magickal, often brutal veil where all forms of magick met and intertwined.

Within that dark plane monstrous, dark beings existed, raged and fed on the fear and blood of others as they fought to escape Shadow Hell. It was a place that raged with terror and echoed with the screams of agony.

Once there, with no memory of their Sorceresses or their abilities to defend themselves, the great winged lions had nearly perished as they faced trial after trial, battle after battle, and roared out in rage as they were killed one by one, until only a few were left. Finally struggling free, those that remained had found themselves within the human realm, and at their less-than-tender mercies.

Queen Amoria's grandmother had found the first Griffon, a fragile cub near death and missing part of its downy-covered wing. Knowing its mother must be near, she had gathered her Sorceresses together, slipped into the human realm, and found not just the mother, wounded and near death, but also two other cubs.

Over the course of several years, using her power as the Guardian of the Lands, and combining it with her magickal Keeper Sorceresses' powers, she had called yet more to her.

Leading them across the Abysmal Causeway that separated magick from human, she had gathered each Griffon her magick could find and brought them home.

After more than half a century, the Griffons were finally home, despite the betrayal of the Wizards and the cruelty of the humans who found them.

Wizards had betrayed their Sorceresses throughout history as well. With the Wizards' arrival in Covenan, betrayal had come to the Sorceresses once again, and to the Griffons as well. Though this betrayal had come in the form of a trusted and revered Justice known for her wisdom and compassion, still many believed it was spawned by the Wizards.

Gods, what evil could have been strong enough to turn her from the Sorceresses she had sworn her magick oath to defend with her life?

And what right did she, Astra Al'madere, have to ask such a question? For here she sat, committing an act nearly as treasonous as the one the Justice had committed.

What was she doing? Using both magick as well as the strength of the Unicorn to drag these traitors to safety?

Why did she bother?

Traitors, after all, were put to death, no matter how handsome, strong, or how they drew a Sorceress Keeper in Waiting.

Traitors were reviled.

Especially Wizard traitors.

They were the most reviled of all.

Yet, using all the strength of the magick she possessed, she managed to create a bed of the softest furs in the farthest depths of a sheltering cave. There, nearly collapsing from the effort to drag them to it, she settled them upon the furs before covering them with yet more.

Waving her hand to the fire pit she had created to their side, she willed the wood to ignite, watching as the flames began to slowly lick at the dried tinder before growing in heat and strength to spread its warmth toward the two males. Astra Al'madere, heir to the Keeper of the Power of the Mystic Forests, stared at the Wizard Twins she had hidden from the Justice of the Guardian of Covenan. Lying unconscious on the bed of furs, sprawled in exhausted abandon, they looked almost—innocent.

Cuddled beside them lay the two weakened Griffon cubs, which she still couldn't believe lived.

Rather than lying broken and bleeding on the valley floor once the spell of stone had been lifted, they were intact, breathing and warm, if weak and confused.

Still, they lived.

That feat alone was one she still found hard to believe.

The babe, Tambor, would need to suckle soon. But his little body drew breaths as his wings fluffed against it for warmth. He was no longer lying in pieces. The stone fragments of the statue dark magic had turned him into was no longer crushed beneath a cruel boot.

Candalar, the half-grown male, had been broken as well. Wings and legs busted from his stone body. Had the spell been reversed before his body had been replaced intact once again, then he would not have known warmth, gentleness or caring again.

His last memory before entering the Garden of Nirvana would have been that of pain, and of dark cruelty.

It would have forever shadowed his afterlife.

Instead, he was warm once more, his pale, amazingly strong wings wrapped about the tawny-and-white fur of his developing body as he snuffled at some dream.

They had found warmth between the two Wizard Twins when Astra had found herself too weak to return them immediately to their mother after bringing Rhydan and Torran Delmari into the cavern.

She too was exhausted.

The magick expended to pull the heavily muscled warriors into the cavern, to create the thick, soft bed of furs in which they lay, and warm the cavern with the fire that now blazed at the bottom of the bed had been near more than her strength could bear.

The battle with the Justice Layel for the Emerald Valley, the heavily forested land the Sorceresses had hidden the Griffons in for far longer than a century, had been draining. The others of the Sorceress Brigade had all been carried to the

38

castle on the backs of the great snow owls the warriors flew, too weak to mount and ride the Unicorns that awaited them.

The Griffons, weakened from the spell that had turned them to stone, could do naught now but call out to the missing cubs.

The Griffoness's calls were the most plaintive, pleading with her babe Tambor to come and suck.

Did the Griffoness grieve for her lost cubs?

Mandalae had been calling out to them since the spell had been broken earlier. Mustafa and Malosa, the two grown males, had roared through the valley, demanding they answer. But just as Astra had been too weak to call the Griffons to the cavern to collect the cubs, so had the cubs been too weak to call back or return to their pride.

Instead, they had found warmth against the dark beings who had so obviously restored their fragile, broken bodies. They sought the warmth of both flesh and of magick and would refuse to budge even if she demanded it.

There had been just enough strength left to secure the entrance against any magick searching the land for the babes, or for the Twins. Just enough to give her a chance perhaps to hide them, or to shield them, should Wizard Twins or Sentinel Warriors find them.

There would be no hope for them, or for Astra herself should, the Select forbid, the enraged dragon Garron find them.

And she had no doubt, nay she knew, there were Sentinel Warriors searching for both the Wizard Twins as well as the cubs.

The cubs to ensure their lives.

The Wizards Delmari to take theirs.

Wrapping her arms across her stomach, she bent over as she sat on the boulder near the fire, trying to hold back the pain and the guilt.

What had she done?

She had betrayed all she loved, all she had fought for since coming to Sellane castle at the age of sixteen. She had betrayed them, and if knowledge of it was learned, then she too would lose her life.

A Sorceress had not betrayed her own in over a millennium.

They had especially not betrayed their own for a hated Wizard Twin.

Especially two suspected to be dabbling in the dark arts and conspiring with the enemy in attacking Covenan and now moving into the lands of the Wizard Twins as well.

She had betrayed her own for Dark Wizards. Oh gods, what manner of weak and unworthy Sorceress had she become?

But Griffons could not bear to be close to dark magick.

The thought drifted through her mind, tearing at her heart as guilt ate into her soul.

Lifting her gaze, she stared at the two sleeping creatures cuddled so close to the Twins and felt her chest tighten at the sight. They curled trustingly against them. As though there were no dark magick inside their souls to torment the young ones.

She couldn't believe she hadn't yet sent out a call to the Guardian of the Lands, the princess who commanded them. These two were supposedly responsible for Covenan's missing heir to the throne of Sellane.

And her queen. Her gentle, compassionate Queen Amoria.

The Wizards Delmari were accused of aiding in the abduction of both the princess and their Queen Amoria. Accused of the most foul, most heinous act of the Princess Selena's near death and the death of two of their own Wizards. Even now, two of their Sentinel Warriors were held in chains beneath the castle for having conspired with them, and their remaining warriors were locked within their quarters until their own guilt or innocence could be decided.

Astra had run to the room of her princess when the dragon's roars had rocked the castle and magickal awareness of the crime had been sent throughout the land to every creature of magick that inhabited it. Along with her Queen Amoria, the Princess Selena had been taken from their own castle and these Wizards were accused of having been a part of that abduction.

Two of their warriors had attempted the murder of their own then had aided the Secular attack on Princess Serena, nearly killing her before the abduction.

These Wizards and their brethren alone were responsible. They alone had brought this destruction to Covenan.

And she had known where to find them. Known they were in the Emerald Valley, weak and exhausted, near death. Yet she had refused to acknowledge such a thing to herself. For if she had, then she surely would have betrayed them in her haste to run to them.

Her magick would always know where her natural Consorts hid, she realized. She should have known when she first felt that faint call of the land, pulling her here. The land itself and all magick contained within it would have called out to her to give them aid.

She had known since the day they had flown to the courtyard of Sellane Castle that they would be the cause of her downfall. She had known they would break her heart, that they would sear her soul, and that they alone had the power to destroy her.

And here she had found them, their magick still glowing about the weakened forms of the Griffon babes as they lay, unconscious, their magick spent from repairing the creatures before returning them to their living forms.

The Sorceresses had left the babes as stone, praying to find a way to do just that before returning them from that hardened hell. But none in Covenan had known the spell to repair the damage created by such a dark and perverted power.

She gripped her sword as she felt tears fall from her eyes, felt everything inside her screaming at her to exact justice now. To strike swift and sure while they slept. While they could not strike back or defend themselves with dark magick.

As she struggled to force herself to do as the laws of the land and of magick itself demanded that she do, the eldest, Torran, opened his eyes weakly.

His features were so perfectly hardened and savage, even in sleep, that when his heavy, thick black lashes lifted to reveal eyes the color of the softest spring blue, a cry nearly escaped her lips.

Her tears ran faster, wetting her cheeks, her lips as her breathing hitched and a low, keening sob echoed in her throat. Pain was a shroud of sharpened spikes driving into her defenseless body, piercing her heart, raking her tender soul like the sharpest dagger and ripping through her tender emotions.

Magick lifted from him, the faintest, faintest threads of that gentle, soft blue struggled to lift from his body as his fingers twitched at his side.

Astra gripped the hilt of her sword tighter, fighting to do what she knew her honor demanded.

To strike them before they could strike another whom she loved.

Yet they had repaired the Griffon babes, brought them back from stone, nearly at the expense of their own lives.

That was no dark magick, surely. For the Griffons were known for their purity and innocent magick.

Pain filled his gaze as his features twisted in regret as he watched her.

Aye, he deserved to feel that regret, and so much more. His soul, if he had one, should be writhing in agony at his acts.

"No tears, love," his voice rasped, rough, weakened. Nearly breaking her with the gentle understanding it held. "Do not hesitate, little Sorceress, our forgiveness will follow you."

She bent over, her forehead touching her knees as she felt her body shake with the sobs she couldn't hold back.

Because she couldn't do it.

She wanted to.

She wanted to strike their wicked heads from their bodies, yet she couldn't draw her sword from its sheath.

Even as the thoughts passed through her mind, she knew them for the lies they were. Even the Sentinels knew she could never force herself to harm them, no matter the crimes they were accused.

Instead, as her head lifted, shock tore another sob from her as she realized her magick was weaving with those weakened palest-blue threads struggling to lift from his powerful chest.

He watched her solemnly, as though he knew her every thought, knew every fear surging through her. And perhaps he did. Any Wizard strong enough to attempt to murder one of their own and conspire to kill a princess would have great dark magick indeed.

Magick strong enough to steal any Sorceress' will.

His gaze shifted to the sword once again.

"Why hesitate, beauty?" he rasped, understanding thick in a voice so weakened it barely carried to her.

"Do not speak to me," she cried out, feeling everything inside her rejecting the thought that she could spill this Wizard's blood. That she could dare to strike out at him.

At the same time, everything inside her was screaming that she do just that.

She had spent her magick once just to save them and the cubs. She had spent her magick again to hide them, to ensure that the rage Garron had sent out through the land toward them could not touch them.

Here, within the Emerald Valley, her strongest magick shielding the entrance to the deepest cavern within the valley, she had betrayed herself, her queen, her people.

Still, her shields should have never been enough to hold back Garron's magick and the violence and rage that had fueled it.

"Do not speak to you." He gave a weary breath as his head turned, his gaze finding the unconscious form of his brother mere inches from him.

His gaze then dropped to the fragile forms of the Griffons sleeping between them.

His lips quirked in a somber line as his hand slid to the baby, his fingers drifting over the white wings and tucking beneath them to the soft white fur that covered the fragile body.

The cub turned on his back, still sleeping, wings unfurling out to his sides as he sprawled out in abandon to allow the Wizard to stroke his undefended belly.

How odd. The babes rarely allowed even the Sorceresses to stroke their most vulnerable area in such a way.

Griffons were born with a knowledge that their bellies were the most undefended parts of their bodies. That it was there that they were most often struck and brought from the skies.

Yet Tambor was allowing the Wizard to stroke him, and even slept through the gentle caress.

"He will need to suck soon," the Wizard advised her softly. "He is weak, and will need his mother."

"When he awakens." She wiped at the tears that still fell. "He has not yet gained the strength to go to her, and I am not yet strong enough to do so either."

44

He nodded softly before lifting his gaze to her once again. "You are weary, Astra. Come, lie between us. Let us warm you and rest. Your magick will then return full strength, and perhaps by then, we can repair a bit of the damage in your thoughts of us."

"How, with a Joining?" Mocking filled the tear-stained laughter that was so pathetic it was humiliating.

Because there was nothing she longed for more than to lie beside them, to have them wrap her in their arms and create the bonding that only came when natural Consorts Joined.

"I fear even we could not establish a Joining this day, love." He sighed then. "It would take far more than one small nap to establish the strength needed to give you the pleasure we long to give."

"No lies, Wizards." She feared she could not bear the pain of them. "Rest. Worry for your own strength, for there will be a reckoning soon. And I fear strength may be all that will aid your escape from this land."

The thought of them leaving, of no chance to feel their touch or the caress of their magick, was near more than she could bear.

"How long—" Clearing his throat, he stared around the cavern. "How long has it been since we found the cubs?"

She shrugged, uncertain. "I found you and the babes, chilled and weak this noon, though the battle for the valley was fought two eves past. The land showed me the gifts you gave in repairing their bodies before lifting the spell. I brought you here." She gestured to the cavern. "And wondered at why you did such a thing."

Did her hatred, her disgust at herself as well as them, reflect within her voice?

The emotions tearing through her were chaotic and left her filled with dread.

45

"They are innocent," he said softly, his gaze on the Griffon babes rather than her. "Such innocence did not deserve such a fate."

Should she excuse him for not seeing the shaft of agony he drove into her heart? Did this mean, in his reasoning, that she and the Sorceresses of Covenan were somehow guilty of some crime and undeserving of life?

Could she forgive such a thought in exchange for the actions of saving the cubs?

Nay, she would forgive him nothing.

"What of my princess and my queen?" she demanded wearily then, coming to her feet to pace slowly toward him, to stare down at him, wishing she had the strength to expend her fury. "Were they not innocent enough, Talagarian Wizard? Did they deserve whatever fate you sent them to?"

His head turned slowly. The look on his face—was it guilt or was it horrified confusion? At that moment, how she wished she had the gift of the Justices to divine the truth.

"What say you, Sorceress?" His voice rasped, as if a great illness tore at his throat. "What is this you accuse us of?"

Her chin lifted, but still her tears fell as she stared down at him. Her anger, her certainty that he must lie, that he must know how he had destroyed not just her queen but also her cousin and her friend, drove spikes of agony through her chest.

"Queen Amoria and Princess Serena did naught to you," she stated, painfully aware that she could not strike him down, that she could do nothing but leave and pray to the gods she had the strength to never return.

"Why?" She could not stop the plea from passing her lips. "Why, Torran, would you take them from us? Did you hate the princess so much for denying your request to question men you had given orders to? Was it the fact that she denied you? Did you know how she stood before the Justices, before you petitioned to speak to the accused and raged at them for their refusal?

"That she begged and all but went to her knees before them to allow you the questioning you sought. For what?" she cried out desperately. "So you could destroy her and her mother? Take from us all we hold dear?" She battled back her tears once again. "Ah Torran, fine warrior of Talgaria, how I wish I could drive my sword through your heart for such an evil act." Sobs tore from her. "How weak am I?" She wanted to fall to her knees in shame and pain. "How weak am I to allow you to live when you have taken them from us?"

Her hand refused to pull her sword free. Her arm refused to make the killing blow. All that seemed willing to obey her commands now were her legs. And she used them to turn and run as fast and hard as her weakened body would allow from the warrior who brought her magick alive in a way she had prayed she would never know.

In a way that proclaimed her the natural Consort of a traitor.

As she turned to run, Torran sent his magick, weak at it was, to cover her. To protect her should she actually leave them alone, without her warmth and her tender care.

To protect her.

He could not risk harm to her. He could not allow her to travel alone, with naught to defend her but her own sword.

Nay, not his Consort. His Consortress. The Sorceress destined to be Consort to both himself as well as his younger brother, Rhydan.

The woman created by magick to match him perfectly, to ease the heart and complete the soul of himself and his brother.

As the magick left his body and cleaved to her, he fell back to the furs, his hands clenching in them as he stared at her, ached for her.

Long before, he had known of love, its mysteries and its charms. And much longer before he had known the agony of her belief that he and Rhydan had betrayed all she held dear, he had ached for her.

He had watched her weep as a young child, had watched her plead with a cold and unforgiving mother. Each time, he and Rhydan had sought to comfort her, their spirits holding fast to her, their warmth wrapping around her.

He'd only wanted to hold her. To ease her tears, to ease the pain that raged at her. How it had torn at him and Rhydan to see her pain and to be unable to comfort her with nothing more than the ghostly warmth they had provided.

Then, to feel her pain these past weeks, to feel her magick reaching out to them, filled with such confusion and betrayal, had burned through their souls like a white-hot blade.

Her magick had not been the only one reaching out though. Their power had reached out for her as well. She had the ability to put a stop to the game the Veressi had all but forced them into. Her magick and her place as their Consortress afforded her the power to reveal her place as their chosen one, and as the woman they could not turn from.

Yet she had not used the power to do so.

She had ached. She had raged. She had watched them in anger and in hope and her magick had reached out to them, stroking them, torturing them with need. But she had not revealed herself to them, nor forced them to do so.

And now, she ran from them.

From them, from her fears, her desires and the crimes she had feared they had committed.

Chapter Three

ಔ

Astra wanted only to run.

She wanted only to escape the pain and the knowledge of her actions, the knowledge of the emotions she couldn't contain and feared would destroy her. Destroy her as they had all but destroyed her ancestors.

Run for the curve in the cavern that would lead to the tunnel and then to—freedom?

Nay, there was no freedom.

She was brought up short by the feeling of magick. A sensual, heated caress filled with gentleness and rich with male regret as it stroked along her arm, twining about it. There was no sense of restraint; there was only the sense of regret, hunger and a need to ease her pain.

A need to ease her pain? Their magick wrapped around her, warmed her and, surprisingly, strengthened what little magick she had left inside her.

Swinging around, facing them, her breathing harsh, tears clogging her throat as she stared back at them with a desperation born of the heartache tearing her asunder.

Why could it not be rage? She could have dealt with the rage, she had known its like before, and she had survived it.

The touch of their magick, both their magick, the palest of blue and the darkest of blue, ignited a sizzling reaction within her. As though the spores of magick that filled her being were suddenly coming alive in ways she had never known they could.

Her thighs clenched as pleasure began to slide over sensitive, reactive nerve endings.

Wizard magick, aligned with Sorceress magick, the fusion of the complementing powers suddenly sent pure sensation to wrap about her nipples, to heat her clitoris and awaken the female needs that had lain dormant in her woman's core.

Even more shocking, more frightening in many ways was the prick of sensation at the tightly clenched entrance of her rear. The entrance that Sorceresses had once given willingly and with great pleasure to their Wizards.

She was such a traitor.

A sob hitched from her chest, and she could naught but close her eyes as she fought to convince herself to run. To leave this place and these Wizards.

Rather than running, she stood there, still, silent, feeling her feminine juices slickening her flesh, running from her vagina to lubricate the swollen flesh of her female folds, then to ease from there along the cleft to the entrance she had never imagined she would feel such pleasure at.

Rather than sending out an alarm, she was trying to catch her breath, feeling her magick rising inside her. The aligning she had felt so rejected by, fought so hard to contain, was rising inside her, slipping past all thought of control.

Lifting her lashes, she stared across the great stone room at the Wizards reclining on the thick pallet of furs she had created for them.

The babes had been gently moved, eased to a fur to the side of them, away from the pallet where the sexually charged magick whipped about them.

Torran and Rhydan reclined in the same position she had placed them in earlier, their bodies uncovered, their cocks rising hard and fierce from the openings of their breeches.

Thick, engorged crests throbbed, darkened by their lust. Heavy veins pounded in the wide shafts as her magick—merciful Sentinels—wrapped around the heavy columns, both of them, like a lover's mouth.

Soft green magick weaved from her, flowed over them, cupped their balls and milked their dicks.

Their magick drew her closer, easing her to them as it stroked over her. Dark-blue strands of the sensual, heated power eased beneath the soft silk of her blouse, capped over a nipple and suckled with a damp heat.

As though Rhydan's mouth covered it, his magick licked and stroked, sucked and nipped at the tender tip until she was shaking with the sensations raging through her flesh.

"Why?" she whispered, unable to stop her own hands from sliding to her breasts, her fingers touching the hardened, tight nipples as she felt the magickal caress lick over them as well.

Her breath caught with her pleasure, her knees weakening. For this moment in time, for just this touch she allowed herself to belong to them.

She would be the traitor again when she could think, when she could make sense of so many emotions and sensations at once. Until then, Sentinels help her, she just wanted to luxuriate in it.

"We're too weak to take you," Torran whispered as she was drawn closer, her legs growing weaker. "But we can give you our magick instead, Consortress. Our touch. This pleasure that only our Consortress could know from our magick."

A Consortress could only find the true heights of pleasure in the arms of her Wizard Twins. For a millennium Sorceresses had been denied the chance to know this pleasure. To experience this touch.

A millennium without the worry that the day would come that they would be abducted for it. Forced to have their magick align with Wizard Twins who refused to court them, refused to give them choice.

Torran bit back a groan, the feel of her magick, like a lover's heated mouth sucked at his dick, drew at the sensitive head as a ghostly tongue licked over it, tasted it. He had to bite back a groan of pure rapture at her caress. The thought that for now she was theirs, if only by magick, was nearly more than he could bear.

Bear it he did though, as her magick surrounded the heavy, throbbing crest.

Pleasure was a swirl of pure power tearing through him, the spores of magick that infused every fiber of his being crackled with nearing rapture. A rapture he knew Rhydan was feeling as well.

Her magick was as soft and silken as the purest power. It suckled his cock, washed over his chest and caressed his thighs with shy, tentative strokes.

It nearly destroyed his control. A control both he and Rhydan knew they could not lose.

Rhydan above all felt that weakness. His magick was weakest, the power expended to save the Griffons had taken a toll neither of them had expected.

Her magick sucked at their shafts, the sensation of a wicked, hot little mouth enclosing the thickened head of his cock was by far the exacting pleasure Rhydan could imagine. No other lover had used her magick in this way, nor had any other lover sent their power racing through them. Especially at a time when there had been so little power left within them.

The weakness in their bodies was dissipating beneath the infusion of strength from her magick touch. It was clenching, tightening with the need to move, to bring her to them, to cushion her between their bodies as they took her in truth rather than with magick.

But magick was all they could give.

Magick was all she would accept.

At least for this moment.

52

As Torran's magick centered on her lush, wet pussy, Rhydan sent his magick to capture the second tight, hard bud of her nipple and eased along the narrow cleft of her rear.

There, his magick touched the wet heat easing from her pussy. The slick juices had the feel of a softness finer than silk, a heat more searing than the strongest magick.

Easing those juices lower with the magick touch he bestowed upon her, Rhydan felt his hips lifting, pushing against the threads of her magick as though fucking deeper into the liquid heat of her mouth.

Torran could feel the wetness of her juices against his fingertips as he watched her nearing the pallet, drawn to them as pleasure began to crackle along the magick threads binding them.

She came to her knees between them, her thighs spread as though for the touch of their hands rather than their magick, the long, soft curls of her hair flowed around her as her head tipped forward in sensual pleasure. Spearing his fingers into those curls, he drew her head lower, her lips to his as she whimpered her pleasure.

As her lips touched his he allowed his magick to thicken at her entrance, to work against it as though it were his cock taking the hot, rich depths. In turn, his magick conveyed the sensations, each snug clench of her cunt against the head of his shaft, the spill of her juices along the thick column.

His magick slipped inside her, working slow and easy, stretching the taut little hole as he eased his power into her as he would have eased his cock inside her.

The added pleasure of Rhydan's touch at the tightened entrance of her rear had her clenching on the invasion. Torran had to fight the need to pull her to him, to draw her body over his and take her in truth.

They could take her only with their magick though. And as his magick fucked slowly into the tight depths of her pussy, he could feel the snug sheath clenching further, the heat intensifying as Rhydan's magick invaded the tight, sensitive flesh of her anus.

She was crying between them, her head pulling away, breaking their kiss. She tipped her head back, those curls slipped over her shoulder, teasing him, teasing his touch and his hunger.

Torran felt her pussy tightening further, heard her cries as he drew her to his chest, pulling her over his body to give her a fuller sense of their possession.

Her fingers curled against his chest, little nails raking the flesh sensually. In the thrust of her hips against the magick invading her he could feel her hunger, her need for her orgasm.

And her pleasure.

The pleasure was whipping about the three of them with a fierce, sensual heat, searing in its intensity.

Astra cried out against Torran's chest as she reached with one hand to Rhydan as well. Gripping his forearm, her body so tense, clenched so tight against the magick invading her, she became lost to the implications of it.

Magick slipped deeper inside her, stretching her pussy, her rear, thrusting into her, building her pleasure higher.

Hot. Pulsing. As though their cocks were actually plowing inside her, stretching her, burning her with their possession.

A firestorm of erotic sensations ignited inside her at every point of sensitivity. Like pinpricks of ecstasy. They were blending, each tiny flame of sensuality merging together until it erupted.

Her pussy and her rear clenched on the strokes of magick driving into them. Swollen, hot, the magick cocks worked inside her, worked her.

They fucked her into oblivion.

Into a release that had her arching, crying out to them and begging—

Begging when she had no idea what the pleas were for.

Begging when she knew, ultimately, that they would be the destruction of her.

Chapter Four

❦

Stumbling from the bed of furs, Astra shakily stared down at the Wizards, much weaker than they were even before they had halted her flight from the cavern, and felt shock lance through her.

Her magick had aligned with theirs in ways she could not have believed possible.

Even now, light-green threads of power stroked over their sweat-dampened bodies, eased about their flesh and fought to infuse them with enough strength to protect them should they have need of it.

She was only barely aware of the Griffon babes dragging themselves back to the warmth of the Wizards, as though they sensed the magick upheaval of moments before had now cleared the air. As though they sensed their warmth, and even the magick that filled their own small bodies could be used by the Wizards who had given the last of their power to save their lives.

The Griffons settled back into their spots, sharing their warmth even as they drew from the warmth of the Wizards who had saved them.

How much easier had she gone to the Wizards?

Not once had she questioned her actions, the sanity or lack thereof in lying with them so easily.

How easily she had gone to them.

A simple touch of their magick stroking against her arm and she was panting for them? Coming to them like a bitch in heat and begging for their possession?

Had she no shame?

Had she no sense of honor?

Aye, she could have naught of either; else she would not have found herself here to begin with.

"Why do you acknowledge me, why attempt to claim me now?" How she hated the shakiness in her voice as she confronted them, so desperate for something to hold to that she would allow such questions to pass her lips. "You did not know me for what I was to you when you arrived to find a Consortress of power. Why want me now?"

The question plagued her. It was one that had left her sleepless far too many nights as she shed tears of shame that her Consorts would so look over her when she had felt such a shift within herself from first glance.

"Astra." The conflict tearing at Rhydan was much easier to sense now that his power was so weakened. "We cannot explain this to you now, as much as it pains me. But I swear to you, soon…you will know the truth of many things."

Later. Her life had always been later.

Later, she would be taught the secrets of the Mystic Forests she would one day command the power to.

Later she would learn the details of her father's death and the battle with the humans that there was no record of.

One day —

And 'twas always one day. A day she feared would never come.

And she was so very tired of waiting. Especially when that "one day" was something her Wizard Consorts believed they could have as well.

"Explain now!" She needed something to hold on to. Something to assuage the guilt and the pain plaguing her. "Tell me, Wizards, did you even know your Consortress when first you faced her?"

How she had filled with excitement when she first approached them and felt her magick rising within her. How she had felt certain they would know her. Perhaps court her.

When they had turned from her, she had assuaged her hurt with the certainty that they could have not known. When they had declared their intent to test an aligning of Powers with the Guardian of the Power of Covenan, she had near screamed out her pain.

Surely they could not have known.

"We knew."

It was Rhydan's admission that tore her heart from her chest and left it broken and bleeding at their feet.

A sickness unlike any she had known filled her belly, souring it and leaving her swallowing in desperation to hold back the bile that would have risen from her.

"You knew?"

Later.

Later she would hate this weakness that filled her voice, the confusion, the uncertainty that she could sense filled her expression. "You knew? Still yet you turned from me and declared your intent to align with another?"

The pain was such that it radiated inside her with a force that near brought her to her knees. An agony that stole her breath and pulled a whimper of pain from her lips before she could hold it back.

A whimper she feared she would never forgive herself for.

"We will explain, Astra." Torran struggled to rise from the pallet, his strength all but exhausted, his magick depleting as he collapsed back instead. "Please, do not hurt so, love. Linger for a moment. Allow us to at least ease the pain we've caused."

"Tell me why if you would want to ease my pain!" she demanded, the force of it causing her to clench her fists against her stomach as it tightened with her rising agony. "Tell me now why you would turn from your natural Consortress in such a way to seek another? Am I hideous?" Tears spilled from her eyes. "Am I not a Sorceress a Wizard could find pride in? Am I not one strong enough, brave enough to complement your power?"

How could she be, when even now she stood before them, begging for such answers?

"Your beauty is such that I fear we could never look away, no matter the danger that could stand before us. Your pride and strength are those any Wizard or warrior would die to possess. Ah Sorceress, you are a Consortress for whom a Wizard would kill to possess," Rhydan whispered with such feeling, with such false truth that she would have screamed in agony did the pain not steal her breath.

"Lie," she accused, possessing not even the strength to spit the accusation out to them as she would have wished. "Just as your ancestors lied, my Wizards, so do you. A lie without regret, else you would at least make me less a traitor by giving me something in which to excuse myself once my Guardian learns the betrayal I have dealt her."

"Astra." Rhydan forced himself to sit up, grimacing at the weakness that weighed him down and kept him from his Consortress. "The truth you seek is not yet ours to give. But know if I could, I would give you that and more. What I will tell you now, upon my oath as a Wizard, is that never would we have taken another Consortress. Never would we have turned aside the most precious gift the gods could bestow upon us."

"Lie!"

Astra had to fight not to sob in agony, yet still the tears fell upon her cheeks like the rains oft fell about the great castle she resided as her chest tightened with a steady, fiery ache within her heart.

"You have made me a traitor," she whispered. "My bond with you would allow nothing less than to give all I am to protect you. Because of you I have betrayed my people, their trust in me, and the lives my ancestors gave to free all Sorceresses from the machinations of Wizards such as you. Because of you, I betray even the land whose power I was to command," she sobbed, her breath heaving, her voice thick and heavy with the truth of her betrayals.

"You have betrayed no one. Nothing," Rhydan snarled, the dark blue of his eyes gleaming with an inner fury.

"Because you say it is so?" she cried, her voice hoarse. "What do I say then, my fine Consorts, when your Wizards learn of my deceit? What say they when it is learned I knew where you hid? Aye, even did I aid you when their command was to turn you over to their Justices? What say they when it is learned I did betray those commands? That I betrayed them and their Consortress? They demanded your immediate arrest for the practice of dark magick and the abduction of my queen and her heir and still I turned my back upon them."

Because of them, even now, Queen Amoria and her heir could be facing death. Astra could not believe she had betrayed her aunt and her cousin in such a way, let alone her queen and the heir to the throne of Covenan.

"No, Astra, such is not true." Rhydan struggled to move to her, to leave the bed she had fashioned with such care. She could feel his pain as well as her own, feel his certainty that he knew better than she.

"Aye, such is true indeed," she cried out. "For you I have betrayed even myself for Wizards who could not care so much as to even acknowledge their Consortress when they knew her for who and what she was to them."

With the pain tearing at her, ripping through her, Astra ran from them then.

From them, as well as herself.

But she wondered as she raced from the cavern to the mighty Unicorn awaiting her beyond...

What did she have to run to?

Chapter Five

ဢ

Torran stared at the ceiling of the cavern, glaring at the roughened stone and the flickering shadows of light cast by the candles his Astra had left burning for them.

What foul magick had dared to do as she claimed he and his brother Rhydan had done? What dark art could steal a queen and a princess from beneath the nose of the powerful Wizard who watched over them in dragon form?

Surely only the gods themselves were so powerful?

As the questions worked through his mind like sharpened spikes of deadly truth, the shift of movement against the shadows on the ceiling had him lowering his gaze once more.

There, moving carefully into the deepest reaches of the cavern, were the powerful forms of the two huge male Griffons.

They knew him.

He had found their valley well before the Wizards had flown into the Sellane Castle courtyards several months ago to begin courting their princesses.

He had fought with the great Griffons, Mustafa and Malosa. He had brought the proud Griffoness, mother to the babes, the special sweet it was written in the Wizard books of history the Griffons so adored.

A mix of honey from the feral bees, the pinon nut and sweetened lark cow milk. He had come prepared to gain their trust, as the Veressi had warned him to do. The Griffons were the most treasured of creatures to the proud Sorceress and Keeper of the Mystic Forests of the Power, Astra Al'madere, as well as the Guardian of the Lands of Covenan, the Princess Marina Sellane.

The Guardian of the Lands drew together the separate powers of the land of Covenan, just as the Guardians of the Lands of Cauldaran drew together the powers of the Wizards' lands.

Except in Covenan, unlike Cauldaran, the Keepers ruled the land they watched over as well, and their heirs, usually the eldest daughter, were sent to the ruling house of Covenan to train beneath the Guardian of the Lands until the time came for her to return to her lands and watch over the powers there. That time was usually decided by the powers of the land itself.

When the current Keeper reached the Reigning Age the land would begin to rumble, the extreme power that resided within it would begin quaking beneath it, and it was then the heir would be called home to take the throne.

Over the years it was suspected the center of a Sorceress' power became weaker, reducing her ability to channel and control the magick that flowed through the land.

It was said that the magick of the Mystic Forests, of which Astra was the heir, had been vibrating with the beginning rumbles of magick too long uncontrolled.

He and Rhydan had been sent to Covenan to find the Guardian of the Land, and then to lay claim to their natural Consortress. Raize and Ruine Veressi, Guardians of the Lands and the Powers of Cauldaran, had urged them to find the Griffons first, to ensure the proud beasts' loyalty to them, before entering the ruling lands of Covenan. And now they knew why. Their natural Consortress was a favorite to the Griffons. They called out to her often for attention, and he knew, once she took her throne in the Mystic Forests, several of the younger beasts would do what none other had done since reuniting with the Sorceress. They would follow her to the great mountain fortress she commanded as her protectors.

The oldest of the two male Griffons approached him on silent feet, his great wings folded at his back, his head tilted curiously to the side as he watched the babes as they lay between him and Rhydan.

The youngest of these two would be one that would follow her.

Moving in behind the two great males came the regal Griffoness. Her expression was one of such concern that sympathy tightened his chest.

She was there for her babes.

Even the half-grown male that lay sleeping so soundly would be given to suck this day, though he had been weaned for several years. Such weakness was detrimental to the pride. She would want him strengthened soon.

"It was not the fault of Wizard magick," he assured Mustafa solemnly as the huge male tilted his head and watched him questioningly. "This dark magic is not ours."

The Griffon snorted with an air of male irritation and uncertainty before glancing back at his mate, the lioness Mandalee.

That they understood his words, Torran had no doubt. The great Griffons were by far more powerful than even the Sorceresses suspected. Once, long ago, Rhydan and Torran's ancestors had been the caretakers and breeders of the great Griffons. What they had learned was that as the Griffons grew in age, power and wisdom, they would gain the ability to not just understand but also to speak to those they eventually bonded to. Those Griffons that had perished as the Sorceresses escaped a millennium before had possessed such gifts, but had revealed them only to the Sorceresses they protected.

Even the Wizard Consorts to those Sorceresses had been unable to convince the great beasts to speak to them. Their instinctive magick had sensed the unnatural pairings that had been made and refused to speak to any but those males who had accepted their natural Consortresses.

By then though, there had been no such thing. There had been no Wizard Twins recorded as having given in to a natural Joining rather than one obtained by forced alignment.

Turning back, Mustafa, followed by Malosa, moved to the pallet of furs Astra had made for them. Reaching the pallet, he bent his big head to nudge the cub Tambor back to his stomach before picking the babe up in the fierce, sharpened grip of teeth far larger than Torran found comfort in.

As he moved back, Malosa moved into place and nudged at Candalar to force him awake.

The weakened cub mewled in protest before the lioness snarled at him in warning, the rumble of the motherly summons causing Torran's lips to quirk in amusement.

Torran almost grinned as the immature male roused himself drowsily, too large for Mustafa or Malosa to carry by the nape, but still young enough to need care.

With an irritated little flap of his wings, Candalar forced himself to stand, his heavy limbs shuddering for a moment with weakness before he stepped from the pallet and padded to where the adults awaited him.

"Such babes should have never been attacked," Rhydan said weakly from where he lay, his tone throbbing with the anger they had both felt at the sight of the broken statues, which had once been living, breathing Griffons.

"Raize and Ruine are correct. Those who would protect the Sorceresses as these Griffons would are fair game for whatever dark source has visited this place. The spell we have placed on them to block such magick from making them defenseless once again will need to be strengthened."

They had worked to return those instincts to the Griffons, aiding the Sorceresses' teachings each time they visited the Griffons but also laying a shield of invisible magick at their underbellies to aid them should they need to fly.

Unfortunately, they had been unable to strengthen the babes in such a way, for they had been too young to accept such infusions of magick. Torran hadn't worried though, believing such little ones would not need it, as they were unable to fly.

"And we are to find this dark magick now, how?" Rhydan questioned him, the anger still throbbing in his voice. "We are considered villains in this land, Torran. The farce we began here to reveal the darkness plaguing it has now turned to take a bite of our rears."

Torran watched as his Twin struggled to sit up, the weakness that assailed him from the amount of magick expended to save the Griffons taking a toll physically as well as magickally.

This situation was one they had not foreseen. Their own warriors had betrayed them all, then, just before ending their own lives, those Wizards had made it appear their commanders, Torran and Rhydan, had given the order to strike the Princess Serena.

They were now being hunted as the most vile of creatures, that of dark Wizards.

"We must leave this place," Rhydan breathed out roughly. "Take our Consortress and—"

Torran laughed weakly. "Take our Consortress? Brother, what say you? She would cut our heads from our bodies with the slightest provocation at this moment. Take her? That was never our plan. Our place is now by her side, our responsibilities that of strengthening her power as well as the power of the land she will command."

"It was never our plan to be considered dark Wizards either," Rhydan pointed out with rueful sarcasm. "What choice do we have but to lose our lives, or do we leave her instead? Here? Without us?"

"I will not leave my Consortress," Torran informed him coldly.

"Perhaps you should have thought of that before we allowed ourselves to be drawn into this farce," Rhydan snarled, weak though he was, a measure of strength entering his tone from the force of his fury. "Bedamned Guardians have placed us in a hell of a position, Torran, and we haven't even our lands to return to. Our Sentinel Warriors are now in the custody of the Sashtain Twins and declared suspects in our supposed crimes until our Justices can arrive to seer their innocence or their guilt and there's a bedamned death warrant on our heads."

Justices were known well for their talents in Seering. The ability to look into any individual and to see, or "seer" the truths or deceptions within them.

"Our warriors will be free soon." Torran placed his forearm over his eyes, allowing himself to sink into a place where the light of the candles did not pierce his brain like daggers sharpened by a Wizard's stone.

Never had he known of a time that his magick had been drained to such a point, but then, never before had he tested the healing magick within him to such a point. Repairing the broken stone, piece by piece by speck of dust until the young Griffons were repaired, then reversing the spell of stone, had been no easy task.

It had taken hours upon hours, more than they had been able to keep track of. Hell, Torran could not even remember that moment when he knew the spell had been reversed and the Griffons were once again whole.

"Brother, our warriors can fend for themselves against the Justices, we ensured it. Such is not the case for us. Should we be questioned then our plan, as well as that of our Guardians of Cauldaran, will be revealed to Justices who have already had one traitor in their midst. This we cannot risk. We take our Consortress, Torran, and we depart this place. Our Owls await—"

A flare of light flashed before them, blinding and intense, the colors of the rainbows mixed and hued with bloody rage and killing fury.

"Dare to take another Sorceress from this land, do you! I think not!" The serrated voice of Shadow Hell echoed through the cavern and sent a chill of trepidation racing up their spines.

To say they were now facing death was perhaps an understatement. There was no magick left to defend themselves. There was no sword close enough even should their magick miraculously appear.

Rhydan nudged at his brother only to hear the wearied sigh that slipped past Torran's lips. "Aye, I feel his rage licking at my flesh, brother. I prefer not to face my death if you do not mind. I much prefer to die as blind as I am weak."

Garron, the Sentinel Dragon, paced closer, steam rising from his nostrils, his black eyes reflecting his inner rage in pinpoints of bloodied red as Torran dared to glance through the veil of his lashes.

He was easily eight feet tall or better, his scales leathery and appearing to flicker with steam and flames. Rhydan near shuddered at the thought of the agony this dragon could inflict before he allowed them to die.

"The Queen Amoria and her child, heir to the throne of Sellane." His voice was like an echo from Shadow Hell reaching from the deep to rumble about the stone walls of the cavern. "I would know now where they are held."

Torran lowered his arm. "How I prayed to the gods that somehow Astra was wrong and they had not been taken." He could feel the sadness, the aching regret that settled in his soul at the knowledge of the two revered Sorceresses' possible fate. Had dark magick taken them, then they would never return as they were before they were taken. "This was not by our hand, dragon. At no time did we reach out to harm those of this land."

Steam hissed from nostrils that flared in rage and disbelief. "Say you this when two of your own warriors were there when she was attacked, prior to her kidnapping? When the Secular's blade found her vulnerable flesh and pierced it?"

the dragon snapped, huge teeth, sharp and foreboding making a sound that near had him flinching in fear that threatened to unman him.

Even Wizards knew the power of such a being whose magick was enough that they could call upon this fierce form and maintain it with such consistent power.

"Was not by our order, dragon." Torran didn't bother to sit up. He'd prefer—should he die undefended, as weak or perhaps weaker than the Griffon babe that had slept so close— to show his contempt at his demise by remaining just where he lay.

Apparently relaxed and without fear.

But that didn't stop his flinch as flames expelled from the dragon's mouth, washing over their heads with a heat that kissed their flesh even from that bit of distance.

What manner of magick was this dragon that he could call even the flames of Shadow Hell to do his bidding?

"I was tasked to protect this ruling house." The dragon paced closer, his rage causing the scales that layered his body to rustle, to slide against each other as the magick appeared to gather just beneath them. "Some being has taken her from me, Wizard, and I would know the part you play in this."

"Nay, we played no part in this, Garron." Rhydan lifted his hands in denial of the accusation. "We would not have taken your queen, nor your princess, and we would have never allowed any other to do so if we had known of it."

Garron's nostrils flared again before a dragony smile of such enraged contempt curved his leathery lips. "You allowed many to believe you were here to conquer this land," he suggested with whispery threads of magick rasping his tone. "You chose to have others believe you intended to Join with the Guardian of these lands, the Princess Marina. This was an untruth, was it not, Wizards? You knew all along who your Consortress was."

They felt it then, too late to slam their shields down to protect their innermost thoughts with a magick too weak to aid them at the moment anyway.

Torran closed his eyes and placed his forearm over them once again with a snarl of fury as Rhydan cursed the dragon. Because there was nothing they could do to stop the invasion, no way to counter the magick that slipped through their minds.

When it was over, Torran lowered his arm and stared up at the cavernous ceiling, gaze narrowed, his awareness of his brother's curses still drifting through his senses.

"Leave off the curses you call down from your bedamned Sentinel Select." Garron's blasphemy had them both staring at him in surprise now.

The mockery that filled the dragon was far less threatening now, but the superiority was enough to make Torran wish the dragon had just turned them into baked Wizards rather than mere weakened ones.

"Your Guardians of the Lands are no less conniving than their ancestors were," Garron sighed as he crossed his massive arms—forelegs? Torran wasn't certain which—over his chest and regarded them with eyes that glittered no less with that blood-red hue of death and rage.

"What mean you, dragon?" It was Rhydan who dared to voice the question with a growl of anger.

"What mean I?" The smile that curled about the dragon's lips was one of sarcasm and certain knowledge. "I mean, my erstwhile Wizards, that it was the Veressi who caused the Sorceresses to run across ice-capped mountains and fiery lakes to escape the Wizards a millennium ago. And now they send you to near certain death at this time in their efforts to once again steal the freedoms of women whose strength and purity of heart will always outshine their less-than-pure, much-too-darkened magicks."

"Our Guardians are no practitioners of dark magick, dragon." Torran forced himself to sit up at this insult. "Neither the gods nor the magick of the land itself would allow such a travesty."

Garron rolled his eyes at the protest. "Your Wizards are manipulating dracas without honor—"

If he'd intended to say more, he hadn't the chance. Without fanfare, with no flames, no steam, no hisses or crackles of scales, the Veressi arrived.

One moment the cavern was free of the heavy magick the Veressi carried with them, and the next moment, it filled the stone-enclosed area with stifling force.

"Garron, do you not tire of baiting us?" Was it Ruine or Raize? Only the gods could tell the two apart for certain.

"Never, Ruine," Garron drawled with mockery as thick as the frightful magick the two possessed as he evidently had no problem identifying them. "Where is my Queen Amoria and her heir?"

"Safe."

Steam issued from nostrils that suddenly flared larger and eyes glittered like orbs of fire as the dragon rose by several feet. A fierce and blazing magick filled the creature, suddenly heavier, more stifling than at any time the Veressi had displayed their rage.

"Should we leave?" Ruine questioned.

There was no mockery. No threat. It was a simple question based on the threat the dragon displayed.

"Think you can escape me?" Garron hissed between clenched, sharpened teeth. "Even the gods cannot hide from me."

"Yet you have not found your queen nor your heir," Raize pointed out as he leaned against the wall. "Neither answer to your call, nor can you sense their magick."

Garron's chuckle wasn't a sound of amusement. "And only the gods can shelter a presence so well. Tell me, Wizards, what did the dark one Dar'el promise you in exchange for your treason against the Select?"

The tension that filled the Veressi was nothing less than a display of the highest offense for the insult Garron had paid them.

"Or what did the Select warn us would pass should we not do as they bid?" Ruine asked as both Torran and Rhydan came to instant alert and Garron seemed to still with a sudden shocking alertness.

Magick clashed with magick in a silent battle as Garron suddenly focused on the two. Threads of Veressi magick, all the colors of Sentmar in darkened hues began to flare and circle the two as Garron simply stared at the pair.

Thinner and thinner their magick became until it blinked out entirely and Torran realized Garron had penetrated their strongest shields as easily as he had penetrated his and Rhydan's weakened ones.

"Such manipulations and games," Garron murmured moments later as his size returned to that of merely dangerously threatening rather than murderously huge. "Such secrets and deceptions when you had only to come to me with a warning and the information you held." He shook his massive head as though wearied of whatever game was being played.

"And think you we could be any more certain whom we faced than the Guardian of this land could be certain as she faced the darkest of the sons of our Select?" Ruine questioned the dragon softly. "Even we, the greatest Guardians of Sentmar, can be deceived by one such as he, Garron."

There was only one they could mean, and Torran felt his trepidation rising.

If the rise in Secular violence and dark magick was the cause of the dark one indeed, rather than simply his machinations, then all of Sentmar was more at risk than they had once believed.

The son of the gods, Dar'el, born golden haired and with the purest gaze, held an evil that the land had never known before him. It was written that the clash of dark magick against that of the pure Sentmarian power had nearly destroyed the land, as well as the moons above, before the Select had managed to imprison their most beloved child within the realms of Shadow Hell. And only then, The One had been forced to awaken. The creator of the Select and all of Sentmar had shed his golden magick, filled the Select with his power, and watched as the dark one was sent to the deepest pits of the lands.

"Return Amoria and her heir." Garron didn't demand, nor did he ask. He made a statement of what would occur.

Ruine grimaced at such a thought. "The danger—"

"You will return them and it will be done quickly." The tone wasn't threatening. The red eyes and bared, sharpened teeth were.

Raize stared back at him, stepping forward and drawing the dragon's attention. "The Princess has the power, among others, to shadow walk," he stated then. "She can escape the place where she is held, and collect her mother as well, if she so wishes it. Despite your insistence, dragon, Sentinel Sorceresses do well exist, and your Princess Serena is just such a Sentinel. Just as we are Guardians of Sentmar rather than mere Keepers or Guardians of Cauldaran alone." Raize's tone was laced with arrogance and command now. "Once our Joining with the Princess Serena occurs, our power will increase then to the level of Sentinels as well."

The differences between Guardians and Keepers of the Lands balanced, strengthened and helped direct the lesser Keepers of the individual lands. During times of peace the differences in Sentinel Sorceresses and Keepers of the Power were slight. Yet that difference, in times of war, rumored to be the only time such Sorceresses came into their full power, was great.

Garron chuckled. "How humble you are," he mocked them. "Does it not smite your pride, Wizards, to know you must have a Sorceress accept you willingly into a Joining to achieve such power?"

Ruine's lips quirked at the irony before he replied, "I believe, Garron, the thought of being truly wanted, needed for that other than our power, we would find greatly refreshing."

Torran felt shock sear him, as well as the sheer surprise that filled Rhydan. No Sorceress had ever been able to shadow walk without help, nor had ever, at any time in recorded history, been called Guardian. If one Sorceress had such power, then it would be a power that would rival even the Guardians of the Lands of Sentmar, the Veressi Twins. The Veressi could only shadow walk with each other's help, even when they walked alone, they drew on their Twin's power to do so.

"I would know if she held such magick," Garron snapped, his black gaze narrowing at the suspected deceit.

"Even if she hid it from herself?" Ruine asked before pushing his fingers through the long blue-black of his hair as his expression tightened with savage intensity. "Our only wish is to make up for the acts our ancestors nearly destroyed the planet with. It is only our desire, Wizard, to ensure our greatest treasure, a gift even our gods could not bestow upon us, lives to fulfill the destiny the magick of Sentmar itself has offered her. A destiny she must find on her own."

This could not be. It was the gods who bestowed the powers. They or the One, the greatest Sorcerer of Sentmar. A creature of such legend that even Garron did not believe in his existence.

Torran glanced at his brother, shock manifesting itself, burning between them as they turned back to the Keepers of the Lands of Sentmar. They were the greatest power on the planet, unless Princess Serena was indeed a shadow walker Guardian.

"I would know, even if she hid such from herself," Garron growled.

Ruine shook his head slowly. "When she was but coming into the power she now wields so effortlessly, we met her in the shadow realms, dragon. There, with Wizards who lived for adventure at her back, she battled the beasts that roamed there with a careless grin and a gleam of adventure in her eyes. Until one day, she no longer arrived within those shadowed lands. Her sword no longer tasted blood and her laughter no longer echoed through the shadowed vales."

"And she no longer led the Sorceresses she had ridden with," Garron murmured as, once again, his power surrounded the Veressi, seeing whatever it was they remembered. "You covered her back—"

A Veressi Twin nodded. "Always, we have watched out for our warrioress, the one we knew was born to be our Consortress. Even before we stepped into Covenan, we have fought to see her at our side once again, her sword lifted in battle, her magick burning around her. We will not see this until she once again accepts the magick that is hers alone to wield."

Garron breathed out heavily, steam emitting from his nostrils as a growl rumbled in his large chest. "A stubborn one that one is," he said softly. "If she does not want to accept what is inside her, for whatever reason, then she will not. If she entered the shadow realm only in her dreams, and found something there that threatened who she believes herself to be, then she will not accept her destiny easily."

The Veressi glanced away from the dragon just enough that even Torran realized...nay, knew, there was much they were holding back.

"Did you Join with your Consortress before the time of the aligning?" Fury began to build in the dragon once again.

"Do we appear to be fools to you?" one snapped back, offended. "Nay, we did not Join with our Consortress."

"What then did you do, my fine Guardians of Cauldaran?" Garron grunted.

"We are the Guardians of the Power of Sentmar." One stepped forward arrogantly. "Not merely of Cauldaran."

"Have you not yet learned better, Veressi?" Garron harrumphed. "Surely you have already suspected what I know to be the truth? When the Wizards of Cauldaran tore the Guardian of Covenan from her lands and broke her bonds with the power that filled her, you severed your rule over the entirety of Sentmar. Your ancestors, Veressi, lost that power to your line as long as the two lands are separated by the Winter Mountains and the Feral Glaciers. That cannot be undone."

It was a truth all Wizards had finally accepted. Their ancestors had done all they could to break the will of the proud, strong Sorceresses who were given into their care. They had abused the strength and beauty of them, denied the hearts of them, and betrayed the bonds that tied Consorts to their natural Consortresses.

"There are many lessons Wizards have learned over a millennium without the hearts that should have been ours. But the loss of the powers given us as Guardians of Sentmar is not one of the lessons we have learned," a Twin all but sneered.

"And some Wizards have far too much pride," Garron sighed. "Whatever you believe to be true is not necessarily what will be. In any event, we must now find a way to convince this stubborn princess that dreams and reality can indeed merge." His gaze narrowed on the powerful warriors. "Take me to my queen. Do so now," he snapped when they seemed wont to argue. "This is not a matter I will reconsider. You will take me to my queen, or you will learn the power of a dragon's fury in truth."

The Veressi glanced at each other before turning back to the dragon slowly. One, Raize if Torran wasn't mistaken, stepped forward. "First, dragon, there is a debt we owe to the Wizards before us for the sacrifice they made to the Griffons of this valley. They gave the power that was theirs to save the creatures our Consortress, as well, is so fond of. We would replace it, if you would give us but a moment."

The dragon nodded as Torran turned to the Wizard Twins yet again in surprise.

Raize moved to them, his hand lifting, the power of his magick suddenly rising from his palm without a sound and curling from it, moving slowly, easing to Torran and Rhydan and washing over them like the touch of an infant, pure and clean.

The weakened center of their magick suddenly flamed to life, the weakness that had once filled them was no more. The months of dangerous weakness they had faced was suddenly a fear they no longer need have.

They were stronger than ever. Filled with a power they hadn't known, nor expected, as their bodies soaked in the pure effervescence of the land itself.

"A gift, not from our Select, but from the land, the magick that whispered your name as Wizards who would defend it in this battle against the one who would pervert the magick gifted to the children of Sentmar."

Not from the Select, but from the One who created the Select. The One who filled the land with magick as a gift to the children who would have perished without it.

"And what are we to use this gift for?" Torran knew that such gifts were never given without reason.

"Your Consortress, Delmari." It was Garron who spoke. "To protect your Consortress."

"One of the most powerful of all of Sentmar's creatures," Raize said solemnly. "The Twelve of the Sorceress Brigade are heirs to the Keeper powers and aligned with the Guardian of Covenan. You must take her as your Consortress, yet you cannot reveal the plans we have discussed. Should she discover them, she must discover them on her own."

Garron's mocking chuckle was once again filled with contempt as his black eyes glittered with disgust. "You believe you can play with these Sorceresses so easily?"

The Veressi glanced back at him, impatience evident now in their expressions. "We know only what we were warned by the Select to expect. It was their wish that the heirs to the Keepers of the Power of each province of his land and the Guardian of the Powers of the Lands of Covenan must find their trust in the Wizards within their hearts, rather than within any proof of innocence. That trust must exist within them for this battle to be won."

"And what battle do you say we face?" Garron growled, the sound one that would frighten even the denizens of Shadow Hell. "The Select have always controlled their wayward son at those times that he's attempted to escape the bonds of Shadow Hell. They will now as well."

"Unless it is not his escape that they fear the most," one of the Veressi sighed. "Dar'el had definitely found a way to escape his prison, we know this by his attempt to convince others that he was indeed you. That fear is overshadowed by the darkness that has joined him, Garron. A darkness far stronger than he, and one we can neither identify, nor can the Select locate."

A darkness that even the Select could not locate? The thought of such dark power was one that had Torran fearing the future of Sentmar itself rather than just the magick that inhabited it.

"Thank your ancestors for this predicament you now find yourselves mired within," Garron snorted to the Veressi. "Had they not believed they could force what should be given, that they could ignore their Consortresses' demands and still retain their loyalty, then you would not find yourself here, facing a battle you may well lose."

"And what makes you believe we could lose the battle?" one of the Guardians questioned him harshly. "What do you know, dragon, that evidently you have not shared with your Select?"

"My Select," Garron snarled. "Nay, they are no Select of mine. But neither are they revealing all they know to you, my friends. For they know well this darkness you face, and they know well the danger it represents, not just to Sentmar but to magick and the very existence of the Select themselves."

"What say you, dragon?" A Veressi Twin tensed further, his expression turning savage. "There is none who could defeat the Select themselves."

But the confidence the Twins normally displayed had weakened marginally. They wanted to believe what they were saying, but obviously, they did have their doubts, just as Torran and Rhydan had theirs.

"Unfortunately, there is," Garron sighed. "And now, Veressi, you face far more danger than you could have imagined. This darkness would destroy each and every Sorceress this planet calls its own. Destroy them and the magick of Sentmar with the greatest of pleasure."

"Why would any wish to destroy those such as the Sorceresses?" a Guardian Twin shook his head as though in confusion. "Why not destroy Wizards or humans instead?"

"Because it is the innocence and purity of love, the Joinings of Wizard power and Sorceress strength that kept this darkness at bay," Garron explained heavily. "Your ancestors knew this. They knew what they risked when the Sorceresses left Cauldaran and in time they began to believe that their own power, the strength that flowed from them alone, would be enough to hold it at bay." His chuckle was one of bitter contempt. "Such pride Wizard males have, and the Veressi more so than others. How does it feel, Raize and Ruine Veressi, to know your line, those who came before you, may have been the hand that dealt to the Wizards their own destruction? Now, take me to my queen."

The Veressi didn't speak, they instead disappeared.

Just that quickly, with no fanfare, and not so much as a sound.

They left as they had come, taking with them the power that lay like a heavy cloud in the air, but leaving behind them the certainty that they would learn the truth of Garron's words.

And once learning it, they would then act. They were the most powerful Wizards to have ever walked the Cauldaran lands. Wizards many feared walked the line between Wizard honor and dark magick.

Garron turned to Torran and Rhydan then, his gaze narrowing upon them, his great wings rustling against his back. "Protect this one the land has given you, Delmari," he growled. "For surely, should you lose her to dark magick, then you will face more than your own heartbreak and loss. You will lose your beliefs and all you inherited. Guard her well, or we may all pay far sooner than you could imagine."

Then, just as the Veressi had done, he simply disappeared. To see his queen, or to track down the powerful Wizards to ensure he was taken to her, they weren't certain.

What they were certain of was the fact that Astra Al'madere, heir to the Keeper of the Power of the Mystic Forests, was their future, their beloved and their natural Consortress. Of that they were certain, and for that they would fight the Select or the darkest demons of the pits of Shadow Hell.

For that Sorceress they would battle the Veressi themselves, or any darkness known or unknown that they could possibly face.

A Sorceress already stealing their hearts.

Chapter Six

ຣ໑

What could she do now?

As Astra bent over Tripelli's neck and raced for Sellane castle, the huge fortress of the Covenani Sorceresses that sat atop Covenan Mountain, she fought to make sense of the situation she now found herself within and the rising premonition that the coming changes to her life were those that would be unavoidable.

There was no escaping the Delmari, she knew. The Talagaria province they ruled was one of the largest of the Wizard lands, Cauldaran, and was written to have bred some of the most magnificent, arrogant Wizards in the land.

The Sorceresses who had been born of Joinings with those Wizards a millennium ago matched the power of those born of the Veressi province as well. Their inherent stubbornness and depth of power along with the power of the Sorceresses from the Veressi and Verago Provinces had assured the escape of the better part of the Sorceresses who had gathered together to escape over the mountains.

Their power and pride hadn't ensured the survival of each and every Sorceress who followed them over the Winter Mountains, through Spring Valley and the brutal cold that filled the Feral Glaciers. Then had come through the Fiery Sands and the mountains of fire.

The mountains of fire had taken dozens of the older Sorceresses who were unable to move with the same strength and speed that the younger ones had possessed. They had lost many of their wisest Sorceresses in the trek across the streams of melted stone and in the sudden explosions of lava and steam that would erupt beneath their feet.

Once the Sorceresses had passed into the Ambrosia Plains, they had collapsed in grief, knowing they had lost not just beloved mothers, grandmothers, daughters, sisters and dear friends, but they had also lost so much knowledge. Of the six history keepers who had fled with them, only one had survived, and her injuries had not boded well for a full recovery.

She'd lived only months, not near long enough to record the history of the Sorceresses, their strengths and weaknesses, their past and the magick they could command. Even more, she'd had no chance to reveal the secrets of the land the wise women had led them to, a land that she herself had chosen because of ties she claimed to have had to it.

The Sorceresses knew when beginning the trek that the land they would call Covenan held a power that even the Wizards of Cauldaran had been unable to detect. It was a feminine magick, a power that called out to them, stronger with each passing decade that they suffered the forced alignments and the knowledge that they were not with their natural Consorts.

It was a magick that not just called out to them, but one that hid, within all its thick, heavy jungles and darkened forests, creatures whose knowledge of that power was far stronger than the Wizards who were but fledglings in age to them.

Magickal beings that, once discovered, would aid the Sorceresses in ways never imagined.

Or so the Grandmother Sorceress had sworn.

So far, those creatures had yet to be found.

Magick had been found. Great centers of magick that called out to those whose feminine power would become their Keepers. Magick that had once kept the land restless, that sent great geysers of flames and molten stone to burn through the skies. Power that would quake and tremble and shudder through the land as it sought to release the pressure contained

82

beneath it and the Sorceresses of power who would direct it through the land instead.

With Tripelli racing through the Emerald Valley, his neck extended, his hooves pounding against the land, Astra could feel that power just waiting to tremble beneath them. Its only outlet was the receptive center of feminine magick, its only relief that of the most powerful Sorceresses in the lands as they centered it, watched over it and eased it through the land in the form of their use of it.

Once used, the remnants of it no longer amassing in strength, it then flowed back into the land, where slowly it would build again, seek release and call out to Keepers, their heirs and those of their blood to ease it once again.

It was a cycle that repeated year after year. One that they sensed, nay, they knew, was shared by beings who watched from a safe distance, who hid in the untamed, untrekked valleys, and within the darkened jungles and forests. Beings whom Astra could sense, especially in the wild lands of the Mystic Forests that she would one day rule.

She was heir to the Keeper of the Power of the Mystic Forests. Within her lay the power to ease the lands of the Mystic Forests as they rumbled in concert with the eleven other provinces and trembled in fury as they threatened to spew their power from Fire Mountain and destroy the beings who the Keeper there was rumored to have seen more than once.

Twelve Keepers of the Provinces, along with the Guardian of the Lands of Covenan, had managed to harness a magick rumored to be even stronger than the power contained within Cauldaran, the land of the Wizard Twins.

And she suspected the Wizards who now inhabited Covenan were beginning to suspect its great power. She often saw the Princess Marina's Consorts as they walked the caverns, their power sliding into the cracks of the cavern walls only to reemerge moments later and fill their Wizards with confusion.

They were beginning to suspect, but, with her, her Consorts would know the secrets they hid, because there would be no possible chance to ever hide the truth from them.

Astra would one day inherit the throne her mother sat upon, the one that sat directly over the center of the power of the Mystic Forests. In that great land, beneath its mountains and in its hidden valleys were secrets that even her mother, the Keeper of that land, was unaware of. There were beings so majestic and proud, yet so wary and uncertain of those who had trespassed into their lands, that even a millennium later, they had not found the courage to come forth.

Astra had always promised herself that once she had taken her throne then she would seek these beings out, create alliances with them, and pave the paths for a greater understanding of Covenan and all it held.

Once she Joined with her Wizards, they would know those secrets as well. They would know all that her magick knew, and if they were indeed of a dark design, then they could easily destroy the Sorceresses as well as the land when that occurred.

Tripelli let out a loud, triumphant whinny as they reached Covenan Mountain. The gates to village common swung open as the tower guard's magick released the locking spell set to the great iron gates.

In more than five hundred years those great gates had not been locked until darkness fell.

Now they were locked at all times, and opened only to those the guards were given permission to allow access to.

Bent low over the neck of the great Unicorn stallion, his silken mane flying around her, Astra sped through the gates and allowed the creature his head. He took the curve and sped along the wide stone path that spiraled up the mountain to the royal residence, the Sellane castle fortress that had been built at the peak. Hooves flying, pounding against the stone road that led up the gently sloped mountain, Tripelli ate the distance.

The inclined road was bordered with the village common residences on the down slope of the mountain and terraced gardens, orchards and temples on the rising slope.

Blacksmiths, bakers, dry goods, cobblers and the various businesses that kept a community running efficiently were all located in the flat land just beyond the inside of the gates.

Residences were not allowed within the business section, just as businesses were not allowed in the residential with the exception of seamstresses, cobblers or those businesses run from the homes of the proprietors and requiring little room for customers or clients to stable, stall or tie their mounts.

As the mountain rose, the more exclusive homes of the common became small estates. Larger temples to the Sentinel Select and their children were erected as well—gathering areas for the festivals of the Sentinel Select, the Joined Wizard Twin gods, Augurin, Pherdan and their Consortress the goddess, Musera.

They were said to have been the first to Join. The first to accept the desires and magick needs the One had gifted them as a way to align and combine their powers. They had been rulers as well as Guardians of power at that time. They had used the magick growing in the land in a way that had urged the spores of power filling it to multiply and bind others together.

They had reached such powers that one day they had disappeared before all their people as they gathered to celebrate their Joining day in a golden array of color. It was then that the One had shown himself as a form of shimmering green and gold and decreed that as the first to follow his commands, they would rule from above for all time as the gods of Sentmar.

That had been so many eons ago that time could not even be measured for it. And still, the power of the Select, that first

Joining of Wizards and Sorceresses, watched over them, guided them and so very often played with the destinies of their children.

With the wind streaming through her hair, blowing it back from her face, Astra sent out the magick call to the gate keepers of the royal residence to release the locking spell to the heavily magicked gates that protected Castle Sellane at the top of Mount Covenan.

The Unicorn did not slow as he passed the entrance. Instead, he kept the pounding pace as they shot through the gates, rounded the royal courtyard and took the turn that led to the back of the huge stone castle and beyond to the entrance of the caverns that began as the land sloped once again.

There was no entrance onto the mountain but for that of the village common or the magically secured caverns, which only a select number of Sorceresses had the key to. That select number was the twelve Sorceresses of the Sorceress Brigade and the caretaker.

Astra was heir to the Keeper of the Power of the Mystic Forests on the farthest edge of Covenan bordering the Raging Seas.

She was heir to one of the four greatest powers in Covenan. The Raging Magick Seas fed the Mystic Lands, its waters crashed at the shores of the Mystic Forests and its magick infused the land with the spray of the surf and the rains that sped in from the vast waters that were infused with the crystalline magick that fed the magick lands.

As the Unicorn came to jolting stop, Astra vaulted from his back, pulled her sword and sheath from the saddle then turned the great beast over to the caretaker. The wizened old man would remove his saddle and halter so the great beast could graze on the lush grass that grew on the plateau outside the caverns until she or another Sorceress needed him again.

Moving into the tunnels that led to the cavern used by the Sorceress Brigade, deep into the center of that level, Astra fought to center herself and ensure that no hint of Wizard magick corrupted her own.

The reigning Wizard Twins, Consorts of the Guardian of Covenan Power and currently holding the throne until the return of Queen Amoria, invariably attended the meetings of the Sorceress Brigade. They rarely spoke, but they watched, and Astra could feel the invisible tendrils of power that swirled about all of the Sorceresses, always seeking, always searching for information.

There were secrets now that there hadn't been before. Guardian Marina, daughter of Queen Amoria, was strained and drawn since her mother's and sister's disappearance. The search for the two had covered all planes of Sentmar and still, they hadn't been found.

Just as the Delmari Twins hadn't yet been found, despite the Wizard pairs searching the land of Covenan for them. What none of them could expect, what Astra did suspect, was the Griffons had aided the shielding of the cavern where they rested.

The great beasts had no concept of the right or the wrong of the magickal beings who protected them, they only knew protecting their own. And she suspected the Delmari Twins, just as the Sorceresses, had somehow become part of their pride.

But if that were true, then it gave lie to the belief that such magickal beings could sense and were offended by dark magick. And that was no lie, she knew. The Griffons were murderous in the face of dark magick. So how then did that answer the question of the Delmari Wizards? Were they friend or foe? Dark Wizards or no?

The land was a magick that harkened only to feminine magick though, and even then the spell to reveal the secrets that watched them silently from the shadows of the lands had not yet been found. If the Sorceresses could not find it, then neither could the Wizard Twins, surely.

Rounding the path to the last tunnel leading to the cavern, she was brought up short by the sound of male voices raised in anger. Easing to the entrance of the main cavern, she felt her stomach drop in trepidation at the sound of one of the ruling Wizards speaking of none other than the Delmari.

"We sense their magick." His voice grated in anger. "There are moments I can almost sense their location before it evades me like wisps of smoke on the wind."

The fury that reverberated through their voices had dread racing up her back. If they could sense the magick of the Delmari, then finding them, surely, would happen soon.

There was an order to kill on sight, issued by the Wizards Justices, though Marina was certain no Wizard or Sentinel warrior would do so. The thought of trusting Wizards to heed their conscience wasn't something Astra placed much faith in though.

"Even the magick of the land refuses to heed my commands to reveal them." Anger and pain threaded through the Guardian's voice, her concern for her missing mother and sister upmost in her heart and her mind.

"Why hide dark magick?" one of the Twins questioned, as confused by such a thing as Astra, and no doubt as confused as his Consort as well.

"I don't know, Caise." Guardian Marina's voice lowered, uncertainty filling it. "Why hide Mother and Serena from me when I whisper my greatest pleas? My power builds daily with our Joining. I can locate any who I think of with the slightest need for their whereabouts and call out to them. All but those bedamned Delmari Twins, Serena and my mother."

Astra felt an edge of relief, sharp and bittersweet as it began to ease the constriction in her chest. Thank the Select that she could not sense the Delmari, for if she did, then surely she would sense their Consortress as well.

"Their warriors know nothing. Our Justices nor yours can seer a conspiracy or hint of knowledge regarding the Delmari's plans or their location. All are loyal to the Delmari though. They'll be searching for them once we allow them to find their way to escape. We've only to ensure they do detect the magick following them, or the Wizards I've assigned to shadow their movements."

Astra's lips parted in shock.

Rhydan's and Torran's own men *would* find them. Their bonds to their Wizards would allow their Sentinel Warriors to locate them, whether the Delmari wished it or no. It was part of the bonds of Wizards and warriors.

She couldn't allow —

She had to fight back the need to rush to Marina's side, to go to her knees and beg for the lives of Wizards believed to be only traitors. Placing her hand tight over her lips, she fought the need to howl out in rage, to beg them to heed the call of her magick and the unknown force inside her that demanded her loyalty to them.

Instead, she backed slowly from the entrance, sent a call to the great Unicorn that had carried her in and rushed back to the exit of the caverns.

She had to warn her Wizards of the warriors who would find them. This conspiracy to trap the Delmari would surely trap her as well. It would doom them all, and the thought of such terrified her.

The caretaker was securing the light saddle back to the stallion's back as she moved quickly into the sunlight, his brilliant-blue eyes filled with concern.

"Is aught about, Sorceress?" he questioned her gently as she gripped the pommel and lifted herself to the unicorn's back.

"All is well, caretaker," she assured him, hoping her quick smile would placate the concern in his gaze. "I merely forgot an important task I was to complete. If the Guardian asks, I will return anon."

Or not at all.

Astra gripped the Unicorn's mane. Giving a firm nudge with her heels, she sent the creature to rise to his back legs before taking off like an arrow from the strongest warrior's bow.

Mane and tail flying, he hit the path down the mountain once more. Astra headed back to the cavern before Delmari Sentinel Warriors drew their Wizards into a trap they would never escape.

The caretaker watched, silent, contemplative as the Unicorn stallion, its golden horn glistening in the sunlight, raced for the exit from the village common.

He would have smiled, but one never knew when eyes were watching.

Such as now.

He could feel the malevolent gaze, the assessing magick as he turned and hobbled to the small stables where grain, rich hay and sweet treats were kept for the Unicorns.

He was careful. Diligent. Always watchful.

Awakening to see the darkness attempting to slip into the lands he'd bequeathed to his daughters had rage pounding at his senses. Learning the magick he'd given to the children of Sentmar was being perverted in ways such as those he saw tendrils of as he walked the land had nearly stolen the careful calm he maintained.

In the centuries he had slept, much had happened. The distance he had been certain would ease between Wizard Twins and Sorceresses had only grown. The distrust his daughters felt toward their Consorts was even greater now than it had been when he had gone to rest.

Pulling his children together once more had been even more difficult.

Ah but the machinations it had taken to ensure Wizard Twins bent their pride and crossed the great frozen mountains that separated them had not been easy.

Thankfully, machinations and the Veressi went hand in hand.

The darkness invading the Sorceresses' lands had spread far further than either Sorceresses or Wizards knew.

Far further than the lovely Astra Al'madere could guess.

Sadness crept inside him, hidden from the watching eyes and the tendrils of magick that sought to learn even the greatest of secrets.

Chapter Seven

ೱ

They were still there.

Rushing into the cavern, racing along the long tunnel that led to the widening cavern at the end, Astra came to a hard, shocked stop.

She stared between the two Wizards, dressed only in the plain, rough silk pants of the warrior made from collin, the material created from the threads of the untamed, unoiled silk worms.

Standing, leaning negligently against the stone wall were the two Veressi Keepers of the Cauldaran Power dressed in black, brushed woven silk, the finest threads created in all of Sentmar, and black blade-skin boots.

The blade—wicked, sharp-toothed, short-legged creatures that inhabited the Causeway, the swamplands between the magick lands and the human lands of Yarba—was prized for its meat and its hide.

Yet it was the dragon that shocked her most of all.

And terrified her.

Had he finally come for her?

Had the magick she knew this dragon possessed finally learned her deceit and come to destroy all that he might suspect threatened the land and the Sorceresses he was pledged to?

But there was no threat, she screamed silently as she stared up at him.

Fear did not hold her before him, still as stone, though it should have.

Nay, it was certainty and the battle to find the words to convince this aloof, vengeful creature that her loyalty was not in question.

Nor were her Wizards.

Proof she did not yet have in her possession. She had nothing but a Sorceress' true knowledge of her natural Consorts, even if it was mixed with a furious sense of betrayal.

Garron tilted his massive head to the side as great dark eyes stared at her with the amused mockery he was so very well-known for. Yet he was not alone in that look, nor was he alone in the massive size and power projecting from him.

There was another, one of dark magick and malevolent design who had been impersonating this dragon whose presence was so trusted by the Sorceresses of Covenan.

Could she be facing the darkness the Sorceresses feared the Delmari had aligned themselves with? Could such be possible? Could she be so very wrong about the Consorts she belonged to?

Surely, the gods... Nay, 'twas the gods who had taught the Wizards—and the humans—all they knew of deceit.

Surely, the most powerful Sentinel, the One, would not have aligned her powers to beings who pledged themselves to the darkness rather than to His almighty hand?

Fingers clenched. The muscles of her body tightened as she called forth the power, the magick the land and the gods of Sentmar had bequeathed her and whispered the words that would call the truth to her.

Not just the truth, but a certainty of whom and what she faced. For she no longer trusted the love in her heart, or her beliefs in others. She had learned better at her dear mother's knee.

The need for certainty was like a dagger slicing through her soul. Calling forth each crystalline spore of power that infused her, knowing that the one who faced her was Garron, then he would know the secret she had hidden since coming into the full measure of her magick. Should it be the dark one, then she and her Wizards would have a chance to escape before Garron and the Veressi could awaken.

Her hands lifted and magick in all the shades of the green of the forest began to surround her. Her hair whipped about her shoulders, caressing her with a warmth that reminded her of her Wizards' touch. Heat engulfed her, infused her, and the spell she sought came from her lips with a strength she had not expected.

"I see a dragon, form and bearing, size and strength of the great Garron. Reveal to me light or should he be dark, magick true and magick deep, friend shall linger, foe shall sleep."

Magick erupted from stone, spilling from even the smallest pores of it, seeping from the ground, exploding in light and fire as it suddenly surrounded the dragon, whipping around him.

Head tilting back, great wings extending majestically, the dragon stood before her. Magick seemed to infuse him, to fly from the stone, the air itself to pour into the dragon instead.

"Garron does not sleep when his charges face danger, little Sorceress." The sound of power echoed and vibrated through the cavern's walls as mighty scales shifted, hissed and steam emitted from flared, leathery nostrils.

No, Garron would not sleep. He would not leave undefended those he had pledged himself to when they needed him so desperately.

The magick of the land in all its heat and radiant power would have revealed the dark one though, if by chance her magick could have been deceived.

"Sorceress Keeper of the Mystic Lands." Amusement returned to the rasping voice as the magick slowly receded. "'Twas great power you called forth." His huge head turned, his gaze going to the Wizards before returning to her. "I felt no Joining."

She had needed no Wizard to hone her magick.

94

She nearly snorted at the idea before remembering the one small secret she had always held to herself. A secret she dared not acknowledge, even in the privacy of her own thoughts, just in case one of the powerful beings in the cavern should discern it. One she would not tell even her Wizard Consorts unless it was a truth that could ultimately save their lives, or the lives of those she gave her loyalty to.

"There has been no Joining." Bracing her hand on the hilt of her sword as it hung at her hip, she faced the dragon as ire flamed within her. "Can a Sorceress not have power without a male to give it strength? Or are you of the mind that a Sorceress can only exist if Wizards provide her protection?"

A shrug of mighty shoulders had her eyes narrowing. "It has been proven, has it not, Sorceress?"

Sliding her gaze to the side, lips parting as her jaw cocked with the slightest mocking tilt, she gave the dragon a haughty look. "Perhaps the One has awakened and decided otherwise?"

Legend said that his awakening would herald a greater magick bequeathed to the daughters he so cherished, and had gifted to the sons he had created to protect all of Sentmar.

She doubted such a powerful being existed now, but perhaps at one time he had. After all, legend began for a reason, and legend said the Sentinel would awaken when the Sorceresses' need was the greatest.

What better time to awaken than now? When had their need been greater in the last millennium?

"Tsk tsk, Sorceress, fairy tales are for fledglings who have nothing better to do than to dream of all-powerful beings who will rescue them from their lives of tedium and uncertainty." It was a Veressi who spoke, his tone more mocking, filled with such dark humor and lack of warmth that a chill actually raced up her spine.

It was the Delmari she watched though. Watched as their gazes seemed to flare with power at the inherent threat in their Guardian Wizard's tone.

Suddenly, threads of pale and darkest-blue magick began to whip through the cavern, sliding around her, over her, warming her flesh even as she gave her eyes a delicate little roll and chose to ignore them. There were other matters that needed to be addressed. Matters of her Wizard Consorts' safety and the plans of the Ruling Wizards to capture them.

"Your Sentinel Warriors are being freed." She fought to hold back the shudder of pleasure that threatened to race over her flesh at the feel of their magick washing over her.

Bedamned warriors, she had no time for this pleasure now.

"We know this." Torran nodded slowly. "The Sentinel Commander sent the message just before your arrival."

"It's a trap."

A smile almost curled his lip. "We are aware of this as well, love."

Then why in the hell had she raced back here to warn them then?

She had done naught but wasted her time, rather than staying at Sellane castle to aid her Keeper of the Lands.

"Do not call me love." The words snapped from her lips before she could call them back, the agony of her choice tearing at her as she faced that once again they had not needed her. "You are traitors in this land and I have protected you long enough. We must now find a way to return you to your own lands, before you lose your heads." And she lost her own. For surely there was no way to convince Marina, nor her Wizards, that the Delmari were not traitors to Covenan.

She glanced at Garron and knew her own fate was sealed there. He would never keep the knowledge of her Consorts to himself.

Why he had not moved to strike her in retaliation for her treason, she was not certain. He had always been fond of her, but he had been fonder of the princesses, as he should have been.

What was afoot here? The air of suspense and male conspiracy was thick enough to slice with her sword.

"They gave up their lands to come to this place to find their Consort, but you do not see them weeping for *their* choice," a Veressi allowed the words to slip past lips that turned in an arrogant curve.

"No tears fall from my eyes, Veressi. And why should they weep when it was at your command they came into our lands and began this farce?" Her finger pointed back at the warriors she would have called her own. "When they betrayed their natural Consortress when they sought another. Weep they should not, for I have no doubt you will compensate them nicely." It was a sneer that shaped her lips this time as her glare turned on her Wizards.

"Think you I did not know when first my eyes touched theirs that our magick aligned?" she snapped with a surfeit of anger, the fury of their choice beating at her Sorceress soul. "Do you think I did not know the moment I betrayed my own land in saving their worthless dracas hides to have you do this!" Her arm extended around the cavern, indicating the Veressi, the dragon. "What conspiracy binds you that I find you here? Tell me, my Wizards." She turned then to the great dragon. "Mighty Garron and the Guardians of lands, my ancestors fled in fear of their lives a millennium ago. Tell me what foul plan aligns you and has brought you together, in this place, this day?"

Her voice rose. Anger surged through her. Her magick beat through her blood, through each crystalline spore of power that infused her being.

She could feel the Wizard magick racing over her, stroking her, her Wizards' need to soothe her infusing her magick as the Veressi and the dragon watched her as though in surprise.

Her Consorts' magick whispered against her Sorceress soul, urged her to ease, to trust in their magick and a loyalty that came only with a natural Joining.

Yet how could she trust? How could she trust two who refused to trust in her? To give her the truth of the conspiracies she felt weaving about the cavern.

"They knew you to be their Consortress." One of the Veressi stepped forward, black eyes solemn, the lean, powerful form filled with certain arrogance and power. "They did what was needed to reveal the Justice Layel before she could kill your Guardian of Covenan and steal the power of this land forever, Sorceress. That deserves more than your outrage."

"We do not need you to stand for us before our own Consort, Guardian," Torran spoke up, his tone a rasp of ire as she faced him and his Twin. "We do not need explanations from you. If her magick has revealed what she claims, then well she should know whether she can find faith in us by now."

She did not know the reasons, no matter her attempts to scrye them. But what of her own actions? The reasons for them tore at her with a dagger of guilt, slicing at her soul as she faced the Wizards she had chosen over her people, her lands and her freedom.

No matter their innocence in the betrayal of the magick of the lands. Still, they had betrayed her in seeking another.

"It was such machinations that drove our Sorceresses from their Wizards so many centuries ago." She bled with pain, with guilt and fear of the rising emotions overtaking her. "Forcing Sorceress to turn against Sorceress, mother against daughter and daughter against sister. It was these games, played by your male pride and besotted egos, that all but destroyed us before we had even the chance to live."

"And perhaps, Sorceress, it was this distrust of their own power that the Sorceresses lent a hand to their own near demise." Garron breathed out behind her. "Deal here with your Wizards, and find that place where truth and lie meet in understanding. When you have settled your choice and decided the side you fight on, truth or confusion, then perhaps your Wizards may reveal to you their own choices, and the reasons for doing so, even in the face of losing the one gift they came to this land to find."

"She would first have to have the maturity to look beyond her own beliefs and believe in the purity of her magic," one of the Veressi sighed wearily before she could reply. "Her ancestors could not do so, and I highly doubt the descendants of those runaway Consortress have matured any further."

"And," the other continued. "I grow weary of the argument concerning Wizards right or wrong. We are but men. Our power is but a part of us and does not make us infallible, no more than it protects Sorceresses from mistakes of their own. What none of our Sorceresses wish to realize is that they have a power much greater than even our own. Now, and a millennium before. Perhaps they cannot see that power, because they wish to be frailer than we. Perhaps their anger isn't so much toward their Wizards as toward themselves and they simply do not wish to realize it."

In a blink, the Veressi were gone. Their magick no longer filling the room, smothering all reason from it as they watched her with chilling disapproval. But she could say she had faced the Veressi with no harm done.

Unlike the stories her mother told her as a child, the Veressi truly were the bogeymen of the dark.

Nay, they were worse, if it were possible to be worse.

Astra turned to Garron then, her arms crossing over her breasts as she stared back at the beast. "So you raised ninnies?" she asked him curiously.

"I would never!" Such an expression of male offense crossed his leathery features and filled his widening, dark eyes.

"Evidently you have." A shrug and lift of her brows indicated her uncertainty. "At least, according to the ever-arrogant Veressi."

A dragony snort emitted with a whiff of steam from flared nostrils. "'Twas not ninnies I raised, my dear Sorceress, 'twas inherently stubborn young women given half truths and partial lies in which to build their futures," he growled. "And I, above all perhaps, wished only to maintain both." He heaved a sigh that lifted his massive chest as he expelled a breath of regret. "For I wished only to maintain the innocence that ensured their kind and gentle hearts."

He turned then to the Wizards who had moved ever closer. "Into your hands I give this Sorceress whose purity is one I have always found solace within. Should it ever turn bitter, aged or filled with regret and pain, then it is I who you shall answer to."

As quickly as the Veressi blinked out of sight, Garron was gone as well, leaving her to face those Wizards, herself and her future, with or without them.

"We have, since your earlier departure, been cursed to have dealt with the arrogance of not just our Keepers but also that infernal dragon. Not just once, but twice. Can you say, Sorceress, that your day could have possibly been worse?" Rhydan questioned grievously. "For I cannot but doubt that it could have been."

Did he now? She knew far differently.

"Truly?" she whispered, the doubts, fears and abject pain of the day assailing her with heartrending force. "Today, I betrayed all I have held dear for Wizards who have already denied me once since they entered the land of the Sorceresses. I have denied my dearest friend, the Keeper of these lands, the truth she had demanded at a time when it seems our very lives are in danger because of your presence here, within Covenan. Tell me, Wizards, which day would you say has been filled with the greater darkness? Yours, in the weakening of your powers and such meetings with arrogant forms? For I can tell you are far stronger now than even when first I met you. Or myself, who must endure the fear of facing the same fate as Wizards suspected of treason, who may or may not be practicing such dark arts?"

Aye, she knew they were not, but her feminine anger would not allow her to voice that knowledge.

"Astra…" Rhydan sighed wearily.

"I believe it is a question I am fully capable of answering," she assured them with no small amount of ire. "For it is I whose day has been the most weary, my Wizards. 'Tis I who must now face those choices, and I tell you now, they are not choices I would have wished."

As far as Astra was concerned, she was finished with this argument, and she was finished with these emotions.

Turning on her heel, slinging off the magick that attempted to slide around her arm, to pull her back to them, she escaped the caverns and the Wizards.

But there was no escaping the hunger, the hurt or the certainty that she would never escape her Wizard Twins.

Lora Leigh

Chapter Eight

ഇ

The return to the castle was made mostly in the dark.

By the time Astra had grabbed a drying sheet and made her way to the bathing caverns, her need for the magick-infused waters was so great she was nearly in tears at the thought of sinking into its heated caress.

The twin moons had risen in the sky not long after she had made her way from the Wizards' cavern. She had watched them rise, full and strong, their once-dimming rings of magick seeming not so hazy as they had in all the years of her life.

It was late enough though. There was every chance the other Sorceresses of the Brigade had already bathed and retired to their suites.

She could not face the small talk that normally filled the evening visits to the bathing caverns. Discussions of the Wizard Twins, who next would become Joined, though all Joining ceremonies of testings of Alignment of Powers had been banned until the Queen Amoria or Princess Serena, preferably both, were returned to their thrones.

Princess Marina had declared the ban in retaliation for the threatened enforced Alignment of Powers by the Veressi with the Ruler in Waiting, Princess Serena, at a time when her mother had been out of contact during her meetings with the Sentinel Priestesses of Covenan.

How things were changing. With the arrival of the Wizard Twins, so much had changed, and Astra was being forced to change with it.

She entered the bathing cavern with trepidation, the uncertainty of facing the other Sorceresses tightening her stomach as the stream and glittering emerald spores of power filled the room.

Steam and the heated waters carried the spores as few other things did, other than the blood of a magickal being.

Bleed, and the bright pinpoints of emerald energy could be seen glistening among the red. The spores infused all that was Sentmar, though it was rumored they had retreated from the human lands long before Wizard Twins had taken their first Sorceress between them.

It was a rumor Astra did not doubt, for it was well known magickal beings could not exist within those lands.

Thankfully, the bathing caverns were empty.

The heated waters bubbled gently about the large pools. The main cavern held six of the large pools. The heated water bubbled from beneath the stone caverns, filling the pools with its magick solace.

With a wave of her hand the warriors' leathers disappeared from her body, only to reappear, neatly folded on a dry stone shelf next to her.

Naked, her body still much too sensitized from the touch of the Wizards' magick earlier in that day, Astra had greatly looked forward to the warmth and solace of the waters. Exhaustion and a saddened realization that she could not stop whatever fate the One had decreed for her, and it seemed that fate was going to be impossible to either avoid or delay for the present, filled her.

Pacing slowly, head down, Astra took the roughly hewn stone steps that led to the magickal caress of the waters. It first lapped her ankles, then her knees. Moving to the smoother, wide ledge beneath the waters, she sank onto the submerged sink with a sigh of relief.

The waters lapped at her shoulders, bubbled around her, caressing her body, stroking against it and reminding her much too much of her Wizards' magick touch. Leaning her head back against the rim of the pool, Astra allowed her eyes to close and beneath the concealing waters her hands drifted languidly over her swollen breasts.

She was so aroused.

So aroused that even now she cursed herself for having left the Wizards. Had she stayed, then they surely would have taken her to their bed. They would have lain against her, sheltering her between them in warmth and in passion.

That Joining could have destroyed her though.

Not a destruction that could harm the land, for everything inside her assured her that there was no darkness in her Wizards. Nay, the destruction would come from the battle and the resentment that would grow once the Brigade and the Guardian who led it learned of her deceptions.

For, though there was no darkness in her Wizards, still, they had conspired with the Veressi, be it for reasons they believed in or nay, still, they had conspired against the Covenan Throne and those who held it.

A crime punishable by death.

It would be yet another crime to destroy such magnificent Wizards. Men whose bodies radiated strength and power. The magick aside, the pure pleasure of every caress, every kiss, every moment of ecstasy guaranteed to be focused solely upon her every need, was near more than she had been able to drag herself from. The promise of a night of sensations unlike any she had ever dreamed was a vow, unspoken yet assured.

She allowed her hands to drift against the sensitive, swollen globes of her breasts, her fingers whispering over the tips of them, near dragging a moan from her as her eyes closed in near ecstatic pleasure.

The remembered heat of the Wizards' touch seared her from her nipples to her womb in such a flare of sensation that it seemed magick itself pulsed to the pit of her stomach and beyond, to her womb.

She would wander farther with her own touch were it not for the sound of leather boots entering the caverns and the sense of another nearing.

Easing her arms to rest instead along the narrow rim just below her shoulders, Astra forced her eyes to open and quickly smothered the irritation that another would disturb these moments she needed so.

"Ah Astra, did you find the creature seeking you this morn?" Aerin Longrieve, heir to the power of the Whispering Mountains, gave a quick snap of her fingers that had her warriors' leathers disappearing from her body.

Rather than reappearing on the clothing shelf just inside the door though, they seemed to disappear entirely. No doubt the maids would find them in the washing room the next morn. The leathers were sweat stained and smeared with grass and mud, just as the knee-high boots had been.

"Sentinels save me from training tomorrow," Aerin groaned, giving Astra little time to answer her question.

Easing into the waters, the black-haired Sorceress found her seat before leaning her head back and closing her eyes on a sigh of bliss.

"There's training yet again tomorrow?" Astra asked in surprise.

It was not often Marina put the Sorceresses through the grueling exercises so frequently.

"She senses something," Aerin sighed, eyes still closed, her voice, though filled with relief, hinting at her confusion. "Shadow Hell, I believe we all sense something that we cannot yet explain."

Astra lowered her head, her gaze focusing on the spores of power that gleamed within the bubbling waters around her.

"You did not say if you had found the creature in need as of yet?" Aerin's head lifted, her brilliant-blue eyes filled with question as she now focused on Astra.

"Not as of yet," Astra sighed.

It was the truth. She had found no creature in true need. The Griffon cubs were already well on their way to finding their strength before she had come upon them and the Twins who had saved them.

"You will return on the morn then?" the other Sorceress asked.

"No doubt they will summon me again," Astra assured her.

What was she to say to such a question? Her conscience raged. She did not wish to lie to one of her sisters-in-arms, yet neither could she tell her the truth.

"No doubt," Aerin agreed with a slight grimace. "When the creatures of Emerald Valley demand our care, there is naught we can do but tend them." A light, fond laugh fell from the Sorceress' lips. "Perhaps it is training as well, for when we have wee ones of our own to tend."

"Let us hope they do not wander to the forests until they are of age to lift their voices and assure us once we are near them," Astra agreed, fostering the belief that the creatures she searched for were being but elusive, rather than the truth as it was.

"Speaking of," Aerin sighed, her gaze turning pensive. "Did you know the Keeper of the Mystic Forests arrived here this day?"

Astra felt her stomach drop.

Fear began to edge through her mind, tightening her body to the point that she felt as though she were facing a coming battle rather than a mother.

"Which suite was she given?" No doubt Astra would be called to explain herself anon. The Keeper could even know, despite the fact that no Joining had occurred, that her daughter's powers had aligned with the Wizards all of Covenan now searched for.

"Think you she stayed?" Aerin's eyes widened in mocking disbelief. "Now, cousin, surely you know my dear aunt and your mother far better than to believe such a thing."

It was often that Astra forgot her mother and Aerin's mother were sisters, so much were they unalike.

Astra shook her head tiredly. "Of course, there is no fortress as fine as that of the Mystic Forests."

Sarcasm shadowed her tone, for they both knew the condescension that filled Alisante Al'madere at the thought of the hospitality of the other Keepers, even that of the Sellane Castle. She felt no other province could match that of her own for power, strength or luxury.

The insult she paid to the queen each time she visited was tolerated only to a point before the queen would immediately send the Keeper back to her own land.

It wasn't Shadow Walking exactly, for the planes used to travel from one province's fortress to the others wasn't exactly a part of the Shadow Planes, but rather a bridge of sorts between each center of power that Covenan possessed.

"Why does she seek you, Astra?" Aerin asked, a bit concerned. "It is not yet time for your year in waiting, and she has made it well known that when your time comes she will attempt to force the land to accept your sister."

Astra's lips twisted mockingly.

Of course she would, and as Aerin stated, her mother made no secret of the fact that it was her intent.

"The land will accept no other," Astra stated confidently, leaning back once again, though rather than closing her eyes, she stared instead at the crystalline spores of magick strapped like emeralds among the stone crevices in the ceiling above.

"True, it will not," Aerin agreed. "But 'tis a betrayal of you, Astra. One you do not have to accept so bravely."

No, she did not, and the other Sorceress' sympathy was near more than she could bear. After all, of all the Sorceress Brigade, Astra was the only Sorceress whose mother wished to break the bond she had with the land. An act that threatened to handicap Astra in the worst of ways, if not destroy her magic entirely.

"The Veressi of centuries before broke a Keeper's bond with her lands and she destroyed herself. You are much stronger than that, cousin," Aerin assured her.

Astra lifted her head and stared back at her cousin with mocking amusement. "They broke her from her lands first. Think you I would allow any to take me from Covenan to begin with? Or allow Alisante to break my bonds with my lands?" With a sharp breath she showed her contempt of such an action should her mother take it. "Nay, Aerin, I will not allow such. As much as I love my dear sister, she will never know the bond with the lands that I know while I live."

Aerin bit at her lower lip, tugging it a second before responding. "What, though, if such an attempt were made upon your life, Astra? Any who would consider tearing asunder the bonds you have with that power would not care to strike out at you with such murderous intent."

Astra narrowed her eyes as the other Sorceress held her gaze. "Think you Alisante would dare such a thing?" she asked. "The land itself would quake with fury, demanding atonement. There is no way to hide such a thing from the Guardian, and Marina would see her life ended for such an act, and all in her line forever barred from holding the power of the Mystic lands."

"True." Aerin lowered her gaze before closing her eyes and leaning her head back against the rim of the natural tub. "She would surely know it was not an act she could hide."

Just as the suggestion was not one that Astra could forget.

It was a question that often plagued her as well.

Alisante was growing more determined with each year to see that her younger daughter, Anja, attain the power to break the bond Astra had with the lands. What they could not seem to grasp was the fact that the hold the land had on Astra was so strong that each year away from it was becoming harder to bear.

"What makes a child unlovable, Aerin?" The words slipped past Astra's lips before she could call them back, just as the tear that slipped past her closed lashes would not be contained.

The hellish years after her father's death, placed in the Village Common of the Mystic Fortress with naught but a nanny who, though fond of the young Keeper heir, still was not her mother, had been brutal. For the other children sensed the banishment, no matter the lies told to excuse the act.

Other parents gazed upon her and wondered what act she had committed that could have been so profane as to cause her mother to cast her away.

And all Astra had known of love had been her tall, strong papa. His laughter and his smiles, the warmth of his arms around her, the strength of his protection had been gone so suddenly—

"'Tis not the child who is unlovable, Astra dear," Aerin whispered, moving until they now sat side by side, her small hand laying against Astra's shoulder in sympathy. "'Tis not the child, 'tis the black heart of the mother and the jealousies of a stepfather. Surely you cannot believe such could ever be a child's fault?"

Astra gave a quick shake of her head. "It changes naught. For it is always the child who suffers, and always the child who accepts the guilt of it."

Moving quickly to her feet, she exited the bathing pool and the magickal waters that were no longer a relief from the aching loneliness she felt inside. She grabbed the bath sheet and wrapped it quickly around her before all but running along the castle halls to find the privacy of her rooms.

As the heavy door slammed behind her, the tears were already falling.

Wrapping her arms about her stomach, she bent over with the pain, sobs fighting for freedom though she pushed them back inside.

Ah gods, why had she returned here? Why had she not stopped along the way? There were many homes in the Village Common where she could have spent the night in solitude, gratefully accepted by their owners for the protection and prestige that one of the Sorceress Brigade would have given their home.

She stayed within the rooms she had been given in the castle rarely in the past year. The sympathy of the other Sorceresses and that of the queen before her disappearance had always been more than she could bear.

For each year, the lands of all the provinces trembled more. Each year the Mystic Forests shifted and vibrated with anger at each act Alisante executed in her efforts to break the bonds her eldest daughter had with the land. And should that bond ever be broken, then one would die. Either Alisante for her treachery, or Astra in grief once the bonds that were all but physical were severed inside her soul.

"Why?" the whisper was torn from her, dragged from the depths of her woman's soul. "What foul creature am I, Sentinels?" she begged. "What transgression did I make to deserve such a cruel, vengeful punishment?"

Eyes closed as she slid along the door until she sat on the floor, she folded her arms against her knees, her head buried against them. She did not see the wavering form of the Wizards who watched her, their expressions torn, their hearts heavy as they fought a battle they were certain to lose.

The battle to ensure she chose their Joining, rather than merely accepting it.

What their Sorceress did not know was that never again could a Wizard Twin force an alignment. Never again would magick merely be compatible with magick, as Wizard Twins had forced in the past.

Nay, Ruine and Raize's father, the former Guardian of the Lands, had ensured that.

Awakened one night by the One, he had told his sons he had cast the spell himself, though the land had accepted it as easily as a Sorceress accepts her natural Consorts' touch.

The spell was taken by the land, held, and as long as Wizard Twins sought out their natural Consortresses, so would those Sorceresses always have a choice. Never again would their magick alone be captured and held, their lonely hearts left barren and unbound. Never again would she be without a choice in who her magick accepts.

From that moment, the magick of the lands and the power of the One combined to ensure the Wizards a chance to once again Join with the women meant for them. But only on one condition.

The Sorceresses must come to their Wizards and accept them freely, or the magick of their Joining would be such that the power she would infuse her Wizards with would be trapped inside her forever. She must reach out to them, accept them, accept their touch and their hearts, or the core of magick trapped within her soul would not open to them.

Yet, to feel her pain, to feel the clash of anger, bitterness and a child's grief as it twisted inside her, was like a serrated blade raking across their bare hearts.

This, their Consortress, was but a woman who ached for all they would give her, and for all they could not gift to her.

They could not force a mother's love, nor return to her the father who had been taken from her. They could not reach into the past and undo all the pain, all the dark, bleak nights filled with her tears.

They could do naught but ensure her future had a far different design.

To do such, they had no choice but to refuse to watch her pain, for in watching, it tore their hearts asunder.

Yet leaving her was not possible.

As they stood to her side, torn between desire and magickal rites, the hazy form of Garron began to waver.

With eyes as black as the pits, his immense dragon form dwarfing the small woman, his expression one of bleak pain, he waved them on their way.

"*'Tis a battle I have helped her fight many a lost and lonely night, my young Wizards,*" he spoke, mind to mind, his sorrow great for this Sorceress he was so fond of. "*See ye well within your cavern until she returns to you. I will see to her inner wounds until such a time.*"

They nodded, grief stricken at leaving her, but lingering long enough to watch as he solidified by her side, the great clawed hand reached out to her shaking shoulder.

She did not have to look to see who reached out to her. Slender arms reached up, gripped iridescent scales and as that hand, a single, clawed hand, covered the delicate, trembling back, she sobbed as a child against a revered father's chest.

A father taken from her long ago.

The father she needed now, much more than she needed Wizards aching to comfort her.

* * * * *

Torran sat with his brother before the fire, a meal of rabbit, brought by the Griffon male, Mustafa, roughened greens they gathered themselves outside the caverns and a flask of wine the Veressi had left with them, their dinner fare.

They could have had much better, but such would have required the use of magick in this land, and would have been trackable by Wizards and Sorceresses awaiting the use of just such magick. Using it for such selfish means as that of feeding the body would serve to reveal their magick much too easily.

The food was barely touched though. It was not the emptiness of their bellies that concerned them, rather the emptiness that resided in their hearts.

And in their arms.

"Such morose figures of Wizards."

Garron's voice had their heads jerking from their plates to the mighty dragon who now stood across the room in all his scaly bounty. He was by far the largest of such forms they'd seen taken by Wizards whose Twins had met an early demise.

Dragons were but small creatures who rested upon the priest's shoulders. Never had one the size of Garron been seen.

"Does she still weep?" It was Rhydan who voiced the question.

Garron harrumphed. "If she still wept, would I be here, Wizards?"

Rhydan set his plate aside as Torran followed suit.

"Beware, Delmari Wizards." He sighed as though weary. "The Sorceress you would take has a battle she must face, and that battle shall come soon. The mother she would have loved attempts, even as we speak, to rip asunder the bonds she has with the land that chose her and conspires to bequeath it to one far too weak to control the tempestuous powers beneath it."

"None shall break that bond." Both Torran and Rhydan came to their feet, their hands gripping the hilts of the swords that hung from their hips.

They would see nothing that Astra called her own taken from her, especially the bond she had with the land. Such a travesty was more than they could bear.

"Be prepared then." Garron nodded slowly. "Be prepared, young Wizards, for the battle may come far sooner than you know."

Chapter Nine

ೞ

Steel rang against steel in the tiny sheltered valley outside the entrance of the caverns leading to the lower levels of Castle Sellane.

The twelve Sorceresses of the Sorceress Brigade and their Guardian Keeper trained beneath the watchful eye of Wizard Twins rather than Sorcerer trainers of strategic magick.

The spore of magick was different within each magickal being who possessed it. As though it attached itself to talents, dreams or instincts and heightened them. Their magick infused those qualities, and gave the one possessing them a far greater sense of that ability than even those who may practice it.

Wizards of strategic or warfare magick could look at the sword, the bearer of the weapon, and see, or sense the warrior beneath whether they be Sorcerer, Warlock, Witch or Sorceress. But even those of the greatest of such magicks could not see the warrior hearts that resided within the Sorceresses as the Wizard Twins who were now Consorts to the Guardian Keeper of the Lands.

"Keeper, get that bedamned sword up," Caise Sashtain roared as the Keeper dropped her guard against his Twin, Kai'el. "'Tis not your Consort you fight at this moment, Sorceress. 'Tis your enemy. 'Tis the Warlock intent on breaking through your magick and tasting that pretty body. Does he do so, what then happens to your magick?"

They were brutal.

Astra sparred against Camry, each aware of the words said even as they blocked what outrage they may have felt for how their Keeper's Consorts trained them. Once they entered the training yard and their Consortress took up her sword, it was as though they were no more than trainers. And their Keeper took no offense to it. Her Sorceresses could sense her amusement, irritation or even her frustration with herself, but never anger or a sense of being dealt unfairly.

Soaked with perspiration, her leathers clinging to her body as the moisture dripped from her hair, stung her eyes and attempted to cool her body, Astra continued to practice the sword with her Brigade sister. Attempted to push back the awareness of her Wizards as they connected with her and aided each quick parry and defensive lift of her sword. As though they whispered what Camry would do before she did so, and then instructed Astra in the proper defense.

They were there with her, lending her strength when she grew weary, knowledge to defend her sword, a gentle touch of something cool against her brow as her magick blazed stronger, brighter within her.

Brace your feet.

That sword is not a babe suckling at your breast. Swing it. Use the strength you've honed and block.

Strike.

Stand firm.

They opened their minds to her, gave her glimpses of their own sword training as young Wizard Warriors, and instructed her in not just defending herself and her Brigade sisters-in-arms but also in the fine art of striking back and forcing her enemy to the defensive instead.

Once she had taken Camry's sword, she collapsed to the grass, eleven swords carrying the ribbons of the house of Al'madere as she panted for breath and swore she could not lift her sword again.

"You have another sword to conquer, cousin."

Astra lifted her lashes, staring back at her Keeper, fighting to breathe as weariness filled her.

Her gaze flickered to the swords she had won that day before she allowed herself to shake her head wearily.

"Verily, Guardian, you are welcome to the swords I have won this day," she panted, exhausted from her afternoon's efforts. "I can barely breathe, lifting my sword would take more magick than I possess this day."

Marina plopped down beside her as Astra found herself forced to quickly sever the connection with the Wizards watching her from afar. She could feel her Keeper's gentle probing of her inner emotions. Not her thoughts, for those were Astra's alone. She searched the emotions of the woman Astra could not hide instead.

"Please, Keeper," she muttered warily, the compassion in Marina's gaze searing her with shame. "I would lose my faith, my strength should I see pity in your gaze."

Astra knew what her Keeper sensed. The torn, jagged emotions of the child who still sobbed inside her soul each time she felt her mother's attempts to sever the bonds the Mystic lands had created inside her, even before her birth.

"What does she do now, Astra?" Marina whispered hoarsely. "I can feel it. I can sense the Land's offense, its insult at what she does."

Astra could only shake her head. How could Marina sense such a thing? Know what even the Wizards she knew to be her natural Consorts had not yet sensed?

"I felt the Mystic Mountains tremble, and for the briefest seconds the rivers churned and threatened to turn direction and spill their magick back to the Raging Seas." Marina's voice lowered further. "The burning rivers that run beneath that land have sent their rage bubbling to the surface, spewing its molten fury from geysers that broke through the very ground itself in several places before she retreated."

Astra sat up, propped her arms on her knees and buried her face in them as she fought to block her Keeper's words.

The feel of that molten rage spewing from the land had brought Astra from a restless sleep before the twin moons had slept and the beaming glory of Musera, goddess of the magickal lands, sent her warming caress to the land of her children.

"Astra, the Mystic Forests give their secrets to you and to your mother alone. Do not force me to demand my answers from the lands that even I can sense crying out to you."

Lifting her head, Astra laid it against her folded arms and stared back at the Guardian Keeper of the Lands of Covenan, sensing, nay, knowing, the Mystic lands were reaching out to her as well now, knowing she would need aid should Alisante continue her treachery.

"What foul act did she attempt to commit against the lands as you slept?" Marina asked again.

"Alisante believed that should she desecrate the final resting place of my father, that somehow his spirit would reach out in anger to punish me for allowing the lands to give up his remains," she whispered, hearing the serrated sound of her voice as the agony piercing her increased at Marina's horror.

"She would not dare," the Keeper whispered in outrage. "His line is descended from the oldest, the most revered of the Wizard Twins. His foremother followed us because her Consorts had passed to the gods, not because of her fear of them. Hers was one of the few alignings that would have been a Joining had she been given a choice."

The purity of that birth, even a millennium ago, had been respected by Astra's ancestors even after leaving Cauldaran. The Sorceresses had a choice in accepting Sorcerers whose magick had also come from such natural alignings so many centuries before, believing it would increase the power of each Keeper of the Mystic Lands. And so far, it had held true.

Astra was believed to be the most powerful yet of her line. Even as a babe she had sensed the magick of the lands she had been born to.

"Anja was with her," Astra whispered. "Alisante forced her to aid her. They tore papa's remains from the magick surrounding him, knowing the land would tell me of their act and believing it would force me to strike out at Alisante."

And had she done so, the magick of the Mystic lands would have no choice but to protect the Keeper it was still bound to. To the woman whose magick was still yet strong enough to command it.

By not striking out, Astra had nearly lost her sanity.

To feel her father's remaining magick jerked from its resting place, torn from the land and then left defenseless within the cruel winds Alisante had called up, had near killed her soul. All that had saved her, and her father's last remains, had been a miracle. Just before that magick had dissipated some force had pulled it from the winds whipping about the lands and somehow secured it. The fact that it was not within the Mystic lands greatly disturbed Astra, but she could feel the security, the safety of her beloved papa's remains for the time being. She contented herself with that.

"Astra, this cannot continue." The voice of the Guardian Keeper spoke.

It was not Marina's gentle tone. It was not a tone of fury, rage or anger. It was one of command, of the certainty that she commanded all magick in the lands, even above those of the Keepers, and she could, and she would, will it to sever its ties with Alisante and flow fully to the Keeper heir.

Astra lifted her head, bowed it, then shook it slowly. "The land must choose."

As she must choose, she thought.

Choose her Wizards or her loyalty to this woman, to one who had sworn her loyalty to Astra years before. And unlike Astra, Marina had never broken her vow.

"The magick of the Mystic Mountains screams out to me in my dreams, Astra," the Keeper revealed. "I will not ignore its cries again, hear you me?"

Astra turned to her once again. "The land must choose to break that bond, Keeper. Should you do such a thing, then it will affect your ability to protect your Keepers of each province for the remainder of your stewardship. You know this."

"I will not see you destroyed," the Keeper swore. "And I would know why you did not strike out at the insanity of her act."

"Because some force, I know not who, heeded my plea to gather Papa's magick and once again shelter it in a place she cannot reach, nor can she find." Astra battled back her tears, knowing that despite the safety of her papa's magick, still, it no longer rested in Al'madere sacred ground where his ancestors' magick had rested for millennia now.

"She won." The Keeper still spoke, that voice of pure power and menace sending a chill down Astra's spine. "She will come for you next, Astra."

Astra shook her head. "She cannot." The land would never remain still for such an act, and neither would the Wizards watching out for her.

"You know Alisante was here yesterday eve?" the Keeper asked then.

Astra nodded. "Aerin informed me as we bathed after my return from the Emerald Valley."

"She returns this eve."

Astra stared back at Marina in confusion at this information. "For what reason would she do so?"

"This information I was hoping you would have." The Keeper reflected at her answer. "For whatever reason, she has requested that you be present as well."

Astra could feel the trepidation feathering up her spine now. She knew the woman who had given her birth well. Deceit and manipulation were but her gentler qualities.

"Must I be present?" Astra asked, suddenly certain she did not wish to be. "I wished to return to the Emerald Valley with Tambor and Candalar again this eve. Mandalee refuses to allow them out of her sight unless I am near, and they are growing weary of her overprotective growls."

"Their return was the answer to all our prayers." It was not the Keeper who spoke with such a gentle voice and such pleasure in her eyes now.

"Aye, 'twas but a dream I could not bear to even consider before we found them," Astra agreed.

She had not told her Keeper of having found the cubs first. Astra had gone to the Emerald Valley with the other Sorceresses and their Guardian Keeper, and was there when they entered Mandalee's lair and found not just the babe Tambor suckling but also the half-grown Candalar.

The nearly adult Griffon had slept even as he suckled, his velvet paws kneading at his mother's flesh as he suckled the magick-rich milk he had been weaned from years before.

"What magick brought them back to us?" Marina wondered. "No matter how I search I cannot find the source."

This was her chance, perhaps. A chance to test the rage inside the Guardian of the Lands toward her future Consorts.

"I sensed Delmari magick," Astra whispered, staring back at Marina and feeling her heart break as rage instantly clouded the Guardian's gaze.

"Never could such a thing be possible." The Keeper was now back. "The Griffons would have given that secret to me, as would the land. Mustafa would have torn them asunder had they come even close to the broken remains of his babes. His hatred of the dark arts is greater than that of any Griffon ever known."

Astra nodded, lowering her head once again. "Aye, this I know. I tell you only what I sensed, Keeper, as I questioned the babes."

She did not lie. She did question the babes, wondering if they would betray her should the other Sorceresses do so.

The babes had shown her that place of dark fear and confusion that had been their prison in their stone forms. They had been cold, as though ice encased them, and Tambor had tried to cry out for his mother's warmth, his father's protection. Their terror had grown until the babe had been close to giving up and searching that path that only the youngest of magicks knew to that place where the Select would gather him to their hearts.

His bond with his mother was strong though, and he'd fought, just as Candalar had done, to find her.

Then slowly, they had shown her how the dark had begun to ease. The glow of life that had begun to fill it.

A sensation of pain nearing, yet it had never touched them.

Astra had realized the Wizards had taken that pain upon themselves.

Not the act of dark Wizards.

It was an act of compassion. Of love. For they had not had to do so, knowing it would weaken their strength even further. Yet neither cub had known even a second's pain as their stone forms were repaired.

The cubs had then shown her of that slow return to magickal warmth. Of little lungs filling with their first renewed breaths. Of sensation returning, tingling at their paws, retracting their claws with a rebirth they had rejoiced at.

Weak though they had been, filled with hunger and confusion, still they had sought the warmth of the Wizards, feeling them as they shared the last measure of their magick with the immature Griffons as they all collapsed from exhaustion.

That was not the act of one whose magick was blackened by evil.

The other Sorceresses had been shown only that feeling of warmth and the return to life. Of warmth and exhaustion. They had, even in their immaturity, sought to reinforce the protection Mustafa, Malosa and Mandalee had extended around the Wizards.

Silence had stretched between them for so long that Astra looked over at the Guardian of the Lands curiously. Marina watched her with a heavy gaze filled with concern, and for a moment, Astra wondered what she sensed.

"I must ask you be here when Alisante arrives," Marina said then, filling Astra with a sense of such shame that it was near unbearable.

To have to face the insanity of her mother's acts was such a travesty that she barely held back her instinctive rejection.

"Might we request Garron's presence as well?" Astra asked then, hearing her voice tremble at the knowledge that there was no escaping whatever cruel and merciless plan Alisante had designed.

"She asks that only you, myself and my Wizards be present," Marina sighed. "But I shall try to ensure Garron is there, if not in all his leathery glory, then perhaps as the invisible shield of protection we have all known when in need."

"What time should I make myself available for the Keeper of the Mystic Lands?" Astra asked with precise respect considered due a Keeper of the Land within Covenan.

"She says she will arrive just after the evening meal," Marina advised her. "I ask that you come dressed as the Keeper Heir of the Mystic Mountains. Give her no chance, no opportunity to weaken your position, Astra. As the two of you stand together, the land you will one day command shall no doubt be strained to hold back its loyalty to you, despite the lack of the ritual giving it over to your keeping."

Astra nodded before rising slowly to her feet. "I believe I will go to the Griffons now then, with your leave, Keeper."

Rising as well, Marina nodded, her gaze compassionate. "Be prepared, Astra. Deceit is something she has honed and now wields with the same strength you wielded your blade this day."

"Nay, Guardian," Astra denied bitterly. "The Keeper of the Mystic Lands wields her deceit and machinations with all the skill and experience of your Wizards should they be forced this moment to defend your life. If only she wielded it to protect the lands, rather than attempting to destroy them."

Marina watched as the Sorceress slowly moved through the training yard, carrying her sword with such weariness she was rather surprised Astra had not left it with those swords she had won for the day.

As much as that worried her, there were other matters concerning Astra that worried her far more.

"She is their Consortress," she whispered as her Consorts drew to her, their magick wrapping around her. "They have not Joined, but you are right. Their magick has touched her and now remains a part of her own to protect her."

"Was the taint of the dark one lingering on her?" Caise kept his voice low, for her and Kai'el's alone.

"There was no taint," she answered, confused. "Weariness, agony whispered across her magick. Fear, a guilt that tears at my heart as though a dull blade has struck it, and the purity of their magick reaching for her, even as hers does reach for them." She frowned at the knowledge of it. "She does not yet realize that to cleave to them, to protect them, is no treachery of her own and her feeling it is tears at her soul. That alone is enough for any Sorceress to bear. But that bitch mother of hers…" Her lips tightened in offended fury. "Were my mother here, she would command I sever the bonds between Alisante and the land and begin the ritual to give it into Astra's protection immediately."

Without her mother's blessing though, the magick of the Mystic Lands would resist, causing a rift between Astra and her lands that would exist until her death.

"What then do you suggest?" Caise questioned her as both he and Kai'el surrounded her, first with their magick, then with their presence as they headed for the entrance of the castle themselves.

"Garron would know of this," she mused. "Continue the search. We tell no one what we sense and see what dark plot Garron is searching for. Could he do so, he would tell me of what is brewing within this mess my Sorceress finds herself within. Until then, we will proceed as though we know nothing of her inner thoughts of those warriors, or the fact that her Joining will come soon."

"She has accepted them then?" Caise asked in surprise.

To that, Marina gave a faint smile. "Can a Sorceress resist her Consorts, do you believe?"

Kai'el snorted in mockery. "I believe, my love, you resisted quite well. I could feel your many rejections weakening my will and my mind."

"Poor warrior." She twined her fingers with his as she reached for Caise with the fingers of her other hand. "'Twas not my rejections weakening your mind, twas but that male arrogance you feared losing. 'Twas not as painful as you imagined, now admit it."

To that, each of her warriors chuckled. The sound was filled with longing, lust and such love her heart was filled to bursting with it. It was a longing, a hunger and a love she prayed the Sorceress now so tormented by mother and Consorts that her heart bled would soon know as well.

For only the gods knew how her tender heart had survived such treachery from a mother, and such loneliness as Marina knew Astra had felt for so very long. And may the gods save the Delmari if they were indeed dark Wizards. Should they betray one who had been betrayed more than any could ever deserve, then Marina swore, even the deepest pits of Shadow Hell would be paradise compared to the hellish existence she would ensure they suffered.

For Marina feared, if Astra were forced to bear more betrayal, her Sorceress' heart might not survive.

Chapter Ten

❧

The feel of her inner conflicts and pain was heartrending.

That evening, Rhydan stood at the mouth of the cave that led to the deeper cavern and watched his Consortress as she ran her hands gently over the soft fur of the baby Griffon that had followed her through the valley to where he and Torran awaited her.

The fact that they waited rather impatiently didn't seem to have affected her just yet.

The fact that she intended to come to them, to Join with them, did not seem to be an act she was rushing toward. Instead, she lingered outside the caves and gave the Griffon babe the attention he was demanding.

Tambor was the smallest of the males in Emerald Valley.

Like any feline, he stretched into each touch, gloried in each caress. Unlike others, the wings that were easily twice the length of his body unfolded, rippled in ecstasy at her caresses, then flapped before he turned back to her, giving a playful growl and attacking her petting hands.

Astra gave a soft laugh before resuming the gentle caresses. She stopped to play when he batted at her hands, then returned to her petting when he purred in pleasure.

She was slowly bonding with the babes in a way that amazed him. Selectra and her sister Solara were the normal caretakers for the Griffon babes, but it was Astra they came to if they knew she was near. And their ability to sense her was becoming amazingly sharp.

Just as his and Torran's ability to sense her was becoming much deeper than it should have been.

He could sense her heartache, her conflicting priorities, her pain at what she believed was his and Torran's deception and rejection of her.

And her guilt.

The guilt that she had not told her Guardian of his and Torran's location. Her feelings that she had betrayed the one she had sworn her fealty to cut into them like a knife.

The Guardian of the Covenan lands and her cousin, Marina Sellane, Consort Sorceress to the Sashtain Wizards, Rulers in Waiting of the Covenan lands until the return of the Queen Amoria or her heir to the throne, was one of her dearest friends. And holding back such information, as well as dealing with the changes evolving in her life, was destroying Astra.

Wizards were ruling the land of the Sorceresses, Sorceresses were now once again Consortresses to the Wizard Twin Rulers of Cauldaran, and there Rhydan stood, wondering how the hell he was supposed to ease his own Consortress' pain. Pain he should not yet be sensing.

Such a bond should not have been possible before a Joining. Before he and his Wizard Twin brother, Torran, had fully taken her and marked her magick for all time.

A magickal being, once Joined, took the aura of not just their magick but also the magick of the one, or ones, they were Joined to. By accepting that magick into herself, she also accepted the fact that her Wizards were a part of her.

A Sorceress, or Consortress, would carry not just her own magickal aura, but it would become infused by her Wizards' aura. The same for the Wizard Consortors. Their aura became infused with the magick of their Consortress, whether she be Sorceress, witch, human, fairy or other magickal being.

"I once knew a Pixie who Joined with Wizard Twins in the Claemai Province," he said softly. "This Pixie had harassed the high-ranking Wizards for years. Their lark cows refused to give milk. Their lands held the last remaining rabbits, which the Twins kept confined and bred exclusively. Those rabbits disappeared over several moon risings, never to be seen again. Fish in their streams began hiding as though too frightened to come out when Wizard magick was near. Even the Snow Owls the Twins rode became skittish. They learned the Pixie, a Sorceress-Pixie Halfling, had come to their land to collect atonement."

"Personal payment," Astra murmured. "Such justice does not exist in Covenan."

But she had heard of it. The practice of exacting payment for crimes that the ruling sect refused to demand justice for. Most often, a crime against a magickal being by a magickal being.

"No, such justice does not exist in Covenan," he agreed, his lips quirking at the thought. "Because feminine justice looks at the law, the breaker of the law, and all the variances that led to that law being broken. They look at the criminal, as well as the victim, and they see beyond simple innocence or guilt."

She turned slowly and stared up at him, the gentle green of her eyes surrounded by the reddened inflammation of her tears and an expression of such conflicting emotions that it only strengthened the powerful response he and Torran were having to her pain.

"What has this to do with what we now face?" she asked, her voice roughened by those tears.

"Much." Moving closer, he eased himself to the ground to sit at her feet, wishing he too could feel her gentle touch, as the cub Tambor had felt.

"Do you intend to explain or must I wait until we are all languishing in the cells beneath Sellane castle?" she asked, confusion and irritation still heavy in her tone.

His fingers moved to the inquisitive cub still begging for affection.

"The Twins went in search of the one causing such havoc. They knew they searched either for a Pixie, or perhaps even one of the fae. They went alone, without Sentinel Warriors to back them, and found the troublemaker at the banks of the stream, masses of fish playing about her petting hands. As she petted, she pleaded prettily that they avoid the hooks, that they make the Twins who owned those lands pay for the sins of a thousand years before.

"The separation of Sorceresses and Wizards had weakened not just Sentmar itself, but the magickal barriers that once prevented humans from abducting the weaker of the magickal beings and forcing them from their lands. That weakening of the magick that had allowed her beloved brother to be captured by humans who degraded him in such ways that when he was found, he refused even to escape. He killed himself rather than be returned to his home where all would know that he was forced to service the humans in their beds."

Few knew the intense pride that the Pixie and fae folk harbored in their much more delicate bodies. A Wizard Twin's pride had nothing on a Pixie's or Fairy's.

"So they found the Pixie and forced a Joining?" she asked.

"Oh nay." He shook his head, the story he'd heard from the Wizards still having the power to affect him. "They knew her the moment they heard her voice, so gentle and filled with pain, with all the dreams she'd known and lost with the loss of her beloved brother. They heard all this in her tears and in her pleas to those creatures given to the land to feed its people, both magickal and not. She convinced these creatures to hide when the magick of a male neared. To only come to feminine magick, to only heed the hooks infused with feminine strength or hunger. The Wizards knew she was their natural Consortress because her pain became their own, her heartache became their heartache. And they knew to take her and force a Joining with such a delicate creature, one of such pride and bearing, would destroy her as well as themselves."

"What did they do?"

Rhydan looked up at her tear-streaked face and sighed heavily. "They did not force a Joining. Instead, they captured the delicate Pixie, brought her to their fortress, and there, allowed her to run and to rule their lives until she realized she was exactly where she wanted to be. A part of their lands and their hearts.

"But still, her pride held her. The Wizards despaired of ever claiming their Consortress. A Consortress they must have though. The age of reconciliation was arriving."

That time when the rulers and land owners of each province must have taken a Consort to ensure chances of conception of an heir before the age of forty cycles. If they didn't, then their lands, their holdings, all but a small recompense was taken from them and given to the heir the Ruler Wizards chose.

"They forced her then?" She couldn't stop the need to feel the cool silk of his jet-black hair as he rested against the boulder she sat on.

His head leaned against her outer thigh as she slid her fingers into the cool strands.

"Nay, they did not force her, even then. They instead gave up. They gave her rule of the fortress and the people who cared for it, and they began their search for a Consortress whose magick could, at the very least, align with theirs. When it seemed they had found such a woman, they then gave their natural Consortress her freedom. The night they freed her, their Pixie came to them. She gave of herself and her magick, and for the first time in a thousand years a natural Joining had been created."

"There's a point to this story, correct?" she asked, the interest in her tone vying with the confusion and uncertainty.

"Patience, my love." He leaned into the deepening caress of her hand in his hair. "There is a point, and I shall give you this point now. That night of an unsanctioned natural Joining, something that had been outlawed in all the land for so long that only our historians remembered the reasoning on it, Wizards all across Cauldaran began to dream of Covenani

Sorceresses, natural Joinings, and the darkness beginning to press against the borders of Covenan. And on that night, Torran and I were captured within the same dreamscape the Veressi were bound within."

Rhydan lifted his head, loath to lose her touch, but needing to see her eyes, to allow her to see the truth in his words.

"That night, my Consortress, I, along with my brother and the two most powerful Wizards known to our race, stood before the One. And he showed us the dark stain beginning to press against the borders of the magickal lands. And he showed us our fate, and the path we must take. He told us we were to tell no Wizard nor man our plans. The Veressi decreed no Wizard, no Sorceress, no being of any plane, magick or otherwise, should know. But you are our Consortress. The other half of us. And you, my heart, should have known long before now."

He reached up to her then, touching his fingertips to her temple, and gave her that dream—the wash of a brilliant light, a warmth filled with pure magick and love, and a voice of gentleness yet booming like the thunder at dawn.

And the darkness, edging across a land He had filled with his magick. A darkness that only the children of magick could defeat.

He gave her this, because she was his Consortress. Not because she had not already accepted them, because they both knew she had.

Nay, he gave it to her to show his trust in her, his link to her, and his knowledge that all along he had known she was his, and all along he had known he and his Wizard Twin would claim her.

"We have always known what you were to us, beloved," he whispered as he allowed his fingers to caress her cheek for a moment.

To feel the sweet, soft warmth of her flesh and to know that finally he and Torran had found that part of themselves they had always sensed was missing infused his magick with a strength even the Veressi could not comprehend.

Sliding his fingers into her hair to cup the back of her head and draw her to him, Rhydan felt the heat and promise of her Sorceress heart reach out to him. To draw her to a kiss, which both Rhydan and Torran knew would seal both their fates to their Consortress, was a need, a hunger he could not deny.

It was a kiss Astra knew she had lived her life awaiting.

Her lips parted for the Wizard who had already claimed her heart, along with his Twin. She knew, as he kissed her, his Twin would feel each touch, each pleasure they shared. He would experience each caress she gave Rhydan and each caress his Twin gave her.

Marina had told her Sorceresses what to expect should they Join with Wizards. The pleasure and magick combined to create such explosive ecstasy, as well as a sense of fulfillment unlike any that could be attained otherwise.

She had also warned them, while their Wizards were present nonetheless, of the reasons the Sorceresses had left their Wizards a millennium before, and of the dangers of the unnatural and forced alignments.

This was no forced alignment though.

This was a true and natural progression of passion and magick of three hearts, three souls coming together in a pleasure Astra knew she could not reject. As Rhydan's lips moved over hers, the heat and velvet roughness of them stroking against nerve endings she hadn't known her lips possessed, Astra reached up, her arms twining around his neck as he lifted himself from the ground.

With his lips moving over hers with hungry force, Rhydan rose above her, bent to her as her head tilted back for him and he gave her a pleasure she couldn't have anticipated.

A pleasure she was unable to combat.

Chapter Eleven

ॐ

Cradling the delicate form of his Consortess in his arms, Rhydan made his way back into the cave, then along the narrow entrance into the cavern where Astra had made the bed of furs for his and Torran's weakened bodies earlier.

Torran awaited them, as did a hundred candles he had conjured, each flickering with a warm, pulsating flame that radiated along the walls. Back from the pallet, a low fire burned, chasing away the chill of the night and the stone that surrounded them, but in the center of the room nothing but heat would surround them.

Laying her on the furs, Rhydan came over her, catching his weight on his elbows as his and Torran's magick disintegrated all clothing that separated them from their Consortess and the warmth of her flesh.

Catching his gaze with hers, holding it as her silken leg lifted to brush against his thigh, Rhydan whispered the words it seemed he had known a lifetime.

"This, our Joining, we take thee as our Consortress," he whispered the old magickal vows of an unsanctioned Joining. The practice of which had been outlawed for far longer than a millennium. "May our aligned magicks blend, merge and create for us the power of three hearts as one, the riches of a life filled with joy and the magick we were meant to share."

As the final word passed his lips, Astra's parted, and he felt Torran's heart leap with his own at the vow she then spoke.

"May the gods bless this magick," she whispered, breathless. "May the One give power to our union and the riches of wisdom to our hearts and our lives."

134

"May we give to our Consortress," Torran then recited, "the pleasure ordained by our gods and gifted by our One. May we, the Wizards no longer of the Delmari lands, now of the Covenan magicks, give all the power of our strength, and all the strength of our love to our Consortress alone."

Magick suddenly blazed around them like a conflagration of rich, vibrant color.

Torran watched the blaze of magick, power and strength, called from the very soul of magick itself, to infuse them, fill them and bind them in ways he knew he would never seek freedom from.

The color of a soft Sentmar green of Astra's magick, the palest blue of Rhydan's and the darkest, deepest blue of the raging seas that Torran possessed began to fill the cavern. It whipped through the room, following that gentle green, only to collide in the center of Astra before striking into Torran and Rhydan.

The colors merged, blended and before invading the three of them became the color of the purest turquoise as the remainder of the vow tore from Rhydan.

"I, Rhydan, now of Covenan, do take thee Astra Al'madere, by right of First Select by Consortess magick."

Right of First Select. The Wizard that a natural Consortress' magick first touched once facing the Twins together.

It had been Rhydan her magick had first touched. It would be Rhydan who would merge his magick, his body with her first.

As his lips settled on her again, Torran's Wizard magick began to stroke and caress her.

Astra arched in pleasure, in ecstatic bliss as sensation piled upon sensation and the touch of Wizard hands and Wizard magick began to possess her.

As Rhydan's kiss became deeper, his tongue licking at her lips, dipping in for long, sipping kisses, his hands stroked down her side to her hip, and Wizard magick began to stroke gently over her.

Gently then more firmly, until all she knew was the pure, rapturous pleasure of a Wizard's magick touch. A breathless moan left her lips as Rhydan's kiss moved along her jaw, then to the column of her neck.

Shivers of exquisite sensation ran through her senses as the touch of Torran's magick began to stroke over her as well. How she knew which magickal touch was Rhydan's or Torran's, still she was uncertain. Yet the pulse of each touch was distinctly different, an incredible flame of sensual, magickal rapture as Rhydan's lips moved from her neck to the hard, engorged tip of her nipple.

As his mouth covered one tight, ultrasensitive peak, the electric heat of magick covered the other as the magick of both Wizards began to caress and stroke her body.

Strands of power wrapped around her, stroked and heated each spore of power flowing through her body as she writhed and arched beneath it. As it wrapped around her thighs, spread them wider and created a cradle for Rhydan's powerful hips, Torran's magick then slipped along the cleft of her rear.

Like the heated touch of roughened male fingertips it drew the juices of her sex back along the hidden entrance between her buttocks.

There, it stroked as she arched, straining beneath the touch as Rhydan's lips moved farther down her body. His tongue licked, tasted her flesh. Turning her head, Astra forced her eyes open to stare at the Wizard whose magick was gently, heatedly working open the entrance to her anus.

"Torran," she whispered his name, drawn to the blaze of iridescent magick that created a hue of dark pinpoints of color that mixed and swirled about her body.

"Ah Consortess," he groaned as his fingers tightened around his cock, his jaw clenching. "Look, love, see where your magick strokes me."

She looked. Her gaze moving down his body to the thick, elongated shaft that speared out from between his thighs.

The broad length of his cock, heavy with his arousal, the flesh dark, the wide crest damp from his passion, throbbed for her touch. Her magick wrapped around it, stroked it as the fingers of one hand buried in her hair, the other braced against the stone wall of the cavern.

Her magick did as she had dreamed nightly of doing for so many long weeks. It surrounded the thick sphere of flesh, suckled and milked it as her magick wrapped around the taut sac beneath.

"In the touch of your magick I feel your mouth, heated and moist, sucking my cock with such pleasure."

Her stomach clenched as Rhydan's lips moved over it.

Her thighs parted farther as magick tugged at them, making room for the breadth of his shoulders. The heated caress of his breath stroked over her clitoris as her hand moved from Rhydan's shoulder, desperate to touch the Wizard whose magick was creating such sensations at her rear.

Moist heat took a suckling kiss of her clit as magick made the first heated penetration of her anus.

The jerk of her hips pressed the hardened bundle of nerves closer to Rhydan's kiss as her fingers found the iron-hardened length of Torran's cock.

Throbbing, thick and hard beneath her fingers, Torran's cock pressed more firmly into her hands. Astra licked her lips, her hips writhing, and pressed tighter against Rhydan's lips as her own ached to stretch around Torran's cock.

The wet heat of Rhydan's tongue stroked against the painfully sensitive nub of her clit. It throbbed beneath his kiss. It became tighter, harder beneath the stroke of his tongue.

The tip of his tongue tucked against the side of her clit, pressed, rotated and sent striking flares of incredible pleasure rushing through the swollen nubbin as Torran's cock pressed deeper into the clench of her fingers.

She wanted him closer.

Rolling her hips into Rhydan's kiss, she tightened her fingers on his cock and drew him closer, her tongue brushing over her lips. Her magick deepened around him, need rolling through her in waves of sensual magick.

"Mercy," she cried out as Rhydan's tongue suddenly penetrated her pussy, pushed inside her and licked with greedy hunger at the juices gathering on his tongue.

The broad crest of Torran's cock pressed to her lips, slipped inside and the magick at her rear thickened and stretched nerve endings that had never known touch, never known possession.

Rhydan's tongue pulled back, then shoved inside again, fucking her with licking strokes as Rhydan, or his magick, she wasn't certain which, lifted her thighs, curved them back toward her breasts and his tongue delved deeper.

Torran's cock thrust hard inside her pussy, pulled back and returned with deliberately provocative penetrations.

She was impaled by magick and heated licks. She was lashed with incredibly sensual sensations, which seemed to ignite each spore of magick inside her body.

"Sweet Astra," Torran groaned. "Your mouth will destroy me."

She drew on the head of his cock, her tongue lashing at it as Rhydan's tongue licked up her slit again, circled her clit and sent clashing, surging sparks of need firing in the depths of her pussy and, incredibly, the tight ring of nerve endings inside her anus.

"My Consortress," Rhydan groaned, his lips lifting from her pussy. "I cannot wait, love."

His voice was hard, hoarse with his need as he came up her body.

Astra was lost in the power of the magick and the sensations tearing through her, but as she felt the press of Rhydan's broad cock pushing between the folds of her pussy, she stilled.

Her lips, wrapped around the hard flesh, eased back, her lashes lifting, her gaze turning back to Rhydan then dropping down his body.

There, the thick stalk of his erection was pressing into her. Spreading her, stretching flesh that had never known possession.

Like a spear of pure heat, Rhydan's dick throbbed at her entrance, then with a hard groan of control lost, his hips jerked and his cock surged inside.

It tore past the thin veil of innocence, drawing a cry of pleasure-pain from her lips as Rhydan fought to still in his possession of her. But there was no stopping. She could not bear it. She needed him. Needed more.

Astra arched into him, driving him deeper. Rhydan's hips jerked again, burying him farther inside her before he gripped her hips, drew back and pressed deeper, harder, burying his full length in a shocking thrust of fiery pleasure.

Sensation became all she knew.

Locked inside her, Rhydan turned, rolling until she straddled his body, held tight against him, his cock buried so deep she was uncertain she could ever forget the feel of him.

Or the feel of Torran moving behind her.

His cock, slickened by his magick and her juices, pressed against the entrance his magick prepared and possessed. The magick eased away, but the sensations intensified.

As Rhydan possessed the depths of her pussy, Torran began pressing into the tight, clenching tissue of her anus. Magick eased and sensitized, lubricated and heated.

Inch by inch the thick length of his shaft took her.

Cries spilled from her lips and Rhydan stole them with his kiss, the taste of her passion still present and infusing the arousal blazing through her senses as she tasted herself there.

She was burning in a fire she could not tame.

She was lost in the touch of a possession she could neither resist nor control.

And she gloried in it.

Gloried in it to the point that as Torran slid fully inside her and the Wizards began moving, thrusting inside her in alternating strokes as they fucked her into oblivion, she knew she would never be the same.

She could do nothing but cry out for them.

Her magick poured from her as theirs poured from them. It collided in a mass of power and strength, whipping around them and blazing like turquoise flames as she moved with them.

As Torren filled her ass, she pressed back, throwing herself into the thrust. As he pulled from her and Rhydan arched upward, filling her pussy once again, she bore down on him, her hips rolling, the blunt heat stroking nerve endings that only stoked the flames of pleasure higher.

She was lost to them.

She was lost in the hunger and the need.

As the strokes became harder, the throb of their cocks stretching her farther, pounding inside her as they fucked her with greedy lust, Astra felt her senses erupt.

The conflagration tore through her. Spores of magick ignited with the pleasure, the possession and the heated penetration of their magick, as well as their release suddenly spurting inside the rich depths of her pussy.

Her orgasm was rapture. It was more pleasure than she heard the Valley of Dreams could become.

It was a wicked, never-ending pulse of liquid ecstasy Astra wanted to hold on to, yet knew she would never survive.

It blazed inside her.

It shuddered through her body and she felt the pulse of their seed spurting with fiery blasts into the depths of her body. The intensity of it stole reason.

It stole all loyalty, all ties and bonds and gave them to her Wizards for keeping.

Just as she had given her passion, her body and ultimately her soul into their possession, she gave them the last measure of herself as well.

She now belonged to her Wizard Twins.

And some last shred of sanity had her wondering just what in Shadow Hell she was supposed to do with them now.

Chapter Twelve

&

They lay upon the furs, perspiration glistening on naked bodies, exhaustion of a truly pleasurable sort wrapping around them.

They lay with their Consortress. Not a Consortess, but a Sorceress Consort. A Consortress.

From their eighteenth cycle they had dreamed of this Sorceress. They had known her name, her face. They had watched her grow into a woman within their dreams and saw the heartache and betrayal of her childhood.

Torn from her home at five and sent to stay within the village common of Mystic Mountain with a loving nurse, she had suffered the knowledge that her mother had sent her away with pleasure. The one who had given her birth had cared for nothing but the land, her duties as Keeper, and ensuring the daughter of her second Consort became Keeper, rather than the daughter the land had chosen.

Her Sorcerer stepfather had cared for nothing but the power to be gained from being with a Sorceress of such power, and ensuring the child they created together benefited from the Joining with the possession of the land.

Astra had grown without parents, with none to nurture that deep vein of love she so longed to give. Even the nurse, despite her fondness of the young Keeper heir, could not assuage her need for family.

Until Astra came to Sellane Castle at the age of sixteen.

Until the Queen Amoria Sellane and the dragon Garron had seen into her aching heart.

Torran and Rhydan had sensed her pain, but their magick refused to allow them to go to her in but the smallest of ways. They were fledgling warriors and she had been but a babe, far too young to understand what her future could hold.

"I was but four cycles when my father died in a battle against the humans."

It was Rhydan who tensed. They both well remembered her fourth cycle, and the agonizing grief of losing the father who had so cherished her. The tall, golden-haired warrior who would awaken her with a gentle kiss to her forehead each morning and take her with him to see to his duties in the village common each morn.

"I awoke to just such magick swirling around me, and believed it was Garron, who came to check on me since the year of my birth, perhaps, seeking to comfort me. It was not Garron was it, my Consortors?"

The acknowledgement of their place within her life filled them both with pride.

Were their chests perhaps extending with a surfeit of that deepening ego?

Torran opened his eyes, his lips quirking at the colors of his and Rhydan's magick covering their Consortress, caressing over her gently. Just as they had attempted to soothe her so many cycles before.

"How were you there with me, even then?"

Torran nuzzled his face farther into her hair to whisper against her ear, "From the night the Claemai Twins Joined with their Pixie Consortress, we have known of you," he reminded her. "You were barely three cycles the first time we, as little more than fledgling warriors, first saw you in our dreams."

Fledgling warriors. They would have been in training. Wizard training began at the warrior stage at the age of ten cycles. Their sexuality hadn't even emerged until fourteen cycles.

A breath of regret escaped her lips. "So many years that you have known. When you came to Covenan, why then did you not at least acknowledge me in some small way?"

The agony of that knowledge had eased, but the memory of it still had the power to give her pause, to ache in some small way.

"And have our magick undo the commands the gods had given us?" Torran asked gently. "We were to aid in revealing the Keeper of Covenan. The one who hid herself so well that even the gods themselves were uncertain which of the two princesses carried such title. To reach out to you would have seen our magick aligning immediately, love."

Aye, that it would have done, for she would not have had the strength to pull back, nor the ability to understand why they would do so.

So many centuries without their Wizards had left the Sorceresses with little defenses against the magickal pull of a natural alignment.

"It does not surprise us though, the strength of the power you wield." Pride definitely filled Rhydan's voice now. And she knew she felt his chest expand as he lay against her.

"Why say you that?" Glancing at him, she caught the amusement that filled his gaze.

"Did you know, little Sorceress, your father, Kalont Vander, was actually a Sorcerer descended from those first Veressi? The Sorceress born of the Keepers of the Lands at that time had conceived just before departing Cauldaran. A Sorceress was born of the union and from that daughter, Sorcerer Twins were born two decades later. Sorcerer Twins carried through your line, did they not? Both your father as well as your beloved uncle died in the battle against the humans that day."

Astra's lips parted in horrified shock. "Say you nay," she demanded.

144

Torran chuckled at the horror. "Ah Sorceress, I cannot say I regret the power, but the inherent stubbornness will no doubt send us sleeping in lonely beds when your anger is roused."

A descendent of the Veressi?

Sweet gods, how cruelly wrong was such knowledge. "Well, I could have done without knowing such. For Wizards many claim to not practice the dark arts, they know far too much about them I would say," she muttered resentfully.

But it did leave open yet more questions, as well as answering others. Now, knowing the depth and the history of her power, she no longer feared the plans she knew her mother and stepfather had for the sister Astra had never truly known. The sister they would force the Mystic Forests to accept as Keeper heir, if possible.

No matter the power her half-sister, Anja Al'madere, may have, it would still have not a chance of challenging her own. The day of reckoning that she knew would come between her, her mother and her half-sister would be not so frightening with this knowledge, or the Wizard Twins she could now call her own, standing at her side.

"Ah Sorceress, how we do know better than that," Torran assured her. "Think you we do not know that the land of the Mystic Forests has been rumbling its discontent for many cycles? That we are not aware that Alisante Al'madere, your traitorous mother, does not seek to see the daughter of her present Consort upon her throne when it is apparent to all that she can no longer control the vast power that resides beneath it?"

How true that was. Alisante Al'madere's control of the lands had been slipping ever more in the past several cycles. Even with the power Anja Al'madere commanded working alongside the Keepers, still it was not enough to hold back the subtle quaking of the mountains that rested at the edge of the Raging Seas.

"Traitorous or no, she is no mother of mine," Astra whispered, no longer resentful, no longer bitter at the loss. "It has been many cycles since I have acknowledged her as such."

"The reckoning will arrive soon though," Rhydan warned her gently. "And when it does, fear not, my Consortress, whether your power will be enough to hold on to what is yours and yours alone. For this is a battle we assure you, you shall triumph in."

That battle, perhaps. But only if she survived the coming conflict, which would see her Wizard Consorts taken from her.

"There are other battles we must first face," she warned them as Torran's fingers stroked against her stomach. "Outlaw Wizards and Sorceresses cannot hide for long in Covenan. Not with Wizard Twins and Sentinel warriors lending their power to our Sorceress Brigade. Controlling the lands of the Mystic Forests will never be if we do not uncover who would see you branded as traitors to Covenan first."

"We must resolve it soon," Rhydan answered her with a resigned sigh. "And we will."

"And how will we resolve it?" Aching fear filled her now. "What do we do, Wizards? We are not just Joined."

"Aye, we love." Rhydan turned to her, his lips brushing against hers as Torran caressed her shoulder with his. "Do we not, Astra?"

She stared back at him, the emotion he had so longed to see filling her gaze now.

"Aye, warriors," she finally agreed. "We love. And perhaps we love far too much and far too deeply. For I do not know if survival would be my fate should aught happen to either of you. What good would I be to the Mystic Forests if I do not have my Consortors by my side?"

There was no warning then. There was no sense of magick or of knowledge.

The intruders were just there.

Eight Sentinel Warrior sets, Twins. Wizard Twins without holdings, property or families of fortune to back them.

And they had arrived.

"Rhydan Delmari. Torran Delmari. Astra Al'madere. You have been found guilty of the highest treason and ordered to be taken into custody and brought before the Ruling Wizards, the Guardian of Covenan and the Justices of the land for judgment against you."

Torran and Rhydan felt her grief as the Sentinel Warriors were followed by ten of the Sorceress Brigade and the very woman they had but been discussing. None other than Alisante Al'madere stood before them, radiant in the colors of the ruling house of the Mystic Forests. The softest green, the most delicate blue and the vibrant gold she had taken with her Joining to the Sorcerer Sol Jol'ante.

The Sorceresses stared at Rhydan and Torran accusingly while the warriors held no expression at all. The Keeper of the Mystic Forests held an expression of triumph though, and a malicious one at that.

Well, perhaps not all the warriors were expressionless. There were four of the Twin sets who watched him with regret, who stared at the warriors of the Veressi uncertainly before turning back to them.

"How did you find us?" Torran asked, knowing the shields the Veressi and Garron had placed upon the cavern should have shielded them.

"A Sorceress Keeper heir cannot hide from the Keeper who gave her birth, no matter the strength of her shields, or others," Alisante stated in her pseudo-gentle tone. "As long as Astra is within Covenan, so can her mother find her."

"Ah, a traitor to your fair daughter once again, Keeper," Rhydan proclaimed, mocking. With a wave of his hand he clothed himself and Astra, as Torran clothed himself as well. Sliding the furs back from their bodies, they rose from the pallet and faced not just their accusers but also the warriors sent to see to their arrests.

Astra's pain was like a stake driving into their hearts as a black-haired Sorceress drew the magick-inhibiting iron cuffs from the belt at her side and stared at Astra, tears filling her eyes.

"Camry—"Astra shook her head slowly. "Do not do this. You know not what goes on here."

"You did this, Astra." Camry's voice was thick with conflict and anger. "This you did when you hid these Wizards and conspired in their escape. Were you innocent of their treason, then you would have come to the Keeper of the Lands and seen to explanations rather than hiding them as you have done."

"They are my natural Consortors," she whispered painfully. "I could not turn away."

"How prettily she lies," Alisante sighed. "How often I have fought to convince Queen Amoria of her lack of ties to the lands and her undeserving status as Keeper Heir. Perhaps this will convince her."

"You lie!" The accusation had each Sorceress glaring back at Alisante.

These were women who had fought with Astra, who had been by her side for the past eight cycles and knew well her connection to the Mystic Forests as well as to Covenan itself.

"The Keeper of the Lands will not abide this betrayal," Alisante suddenly hissed in retaliation. "She cannot ignore what you have done, Astra."

"Anja will not take my place, Alisante," Astra assured her. "The land will not have it. Already it trembles in anger at your attempt to sever its ties to me. Only my death can sever the bonds I have with it."

Alisante's lips twitched in the barest smile of calculating triumph.

Astra felt her jaw clenching in rage. "Ah, so this is your scheme." Bitterness now filled her. "You believe that in delivering me to judgment for crimes not committed that you will see my death? Nay, Keeper, such will not happen. The lands I will soon command will not allow it." As she spoke, the merging power of the Joining, a turquoise as pure and radiant as power itself began to glow about her.

The cavern trembled, the echo of the land's anger at her treatment suddenly filling the room in the colors of the Mystic Forest's power. The blues and the greens swirled up from the cavern floor, wrapped around her, then extended out to Rhydan and Torran as they watched the display in surprise.

Alisante jumped back in fear and shock, her pale face seeming to whiten further as the swirling colors darkened the closer they came to her.

"I will see no such thing," the Keeper snarled, her own hands lifting as power began to pour from them. "I am still Keeper of the Mystic Forests, you little dracas whore."

But her power, strong though it was, could not compare to that which Astra wielded. The power of the Mystic Forests, fused with the Raging Seas, descended by the greatest Keepers ever known, the Veressi, and strengthened by Wizard Consorts broke easily past the guards the Mystic Keeper threw up before it.

Warriors and Sorceresses scattered throughout the cavern.

Rhydan could feel the Sentinel Warriors suddenly combining their powers and attempting to surround him. A move normally guaranteed to negate a Wizard's power.

But Rhydan and Torran had been strengthened by the Veressi themselves as well as their Consortress.

By the very heart of Sentmar's magick.

Taking them would not be nearly so easy.

Connecting with their Consortress, sharing the thought with her that they could easily shadow jump and escape, was their quickest plan. They would not see her judged by a mother's hatred, or the condemnation of the Sorceresses she had fought beside for so long.

"No." She shook her head slowly, using her magick to do no more than hold Alisante at bay. "I can't leave."

A wave of her hand and Alisante slumped against the cavern wall, staring at her own hands in disbelief, unable to accept that the land, that her own magick and her deceit had failed her.

Astra could only stare at the woman she had once called mother. Betraying that poisonous woman would mean nothing to her, but she couldn't betray Marina further. She had already committed the ultimate treason, she would not add cowardice to her crimes by leaving Covenan. It would destroy her.

"Astra, do not make us fight you," Camry pleaded with her. "Come with us willingly. Do not destroy our hearts this way."

Rhydan felt his chest aching with the sob that hitched from his Astra's chest as she faced the women she had called sisters.

"You go nowhere," Rhydan ordered her, the command in his voice heavy with dire warning. "But with us."

Tears fell from her eyes, her lips trembling as her hands clenched at her sides, little fists of desperation and fury as she shuddered with the cries she fought to hold in.

"I will not leave Covenan," she swore, terrifying him to the deepest levels of his being, because to stay could very well mean her life if Alisante Al'madere had her way. And she would hold sway over all but the missing queen.

"Not for long, my heart," he swore. "Just until we have this safely resolved."

"Not even for a moment," she denied, her voice hitching with her tears. "No, my Consortors. I'll never run from my queen, nor my Guardian." She stared back at them, the tears, the pain raging through her staying his hand when he would have forced her to shadow jump with them. "I will be unharmed. Go, the shadow planes will protect you where I cannot."

"Only the Veressi shadow jump," one of the warriors proclaimed.

Rhydan ignored him as he turned back to his Consortress.

"What you face, so shall we," Torran sighed before arching his brows to the Sentinel Warriors. "There will be no chains and there will be no restraints upon our magick. We will go willingly."

Evidently, such an answer was unacceptable to several of the Sentinel Warriors. Before Rhydan and Torran could guess their intent, a powerful, combined surge of magick infused with a spell to painfully disarm not just them but also Astra hurled toward them.

They could not have guessed Astra's powerful answer.

* * * * *

The knowledge of the Joining and the danger pierced Marina's senses, and along with it all the knowledge that her Sorceresses were unaware the Guardian could perceive when Sorceress and Wizard Twins became one magick with Sentmar.

Her head jerked up, her gaze swinging from the charts she had been perusing to the surprised gazes of her Consortors, and that of the dragon Garron.

Black, solemn eyes in a leathery dragon's face seemed to widen, as though he felt the danger and the warning at the same moment.

Her lips parted and Marina couldn't stop the tears that filled her eyes, the ache that tore at her heart. The regret that

151

the Sorceress she was so fond of had been too frightened of the repercussions to come to her.

There was other knowledge as well.

The knowledge of the darkness that sensed the Joining, and its anger over it. The Sentinel Warriors who had sensed the magick, the Sorceresses searching for it, the jealousy and vindictiveness of a mother, and the powers vying to destroy the Joining converging on one small cavern at the edge of the Emerald Valley.

Those of magick were not the only ones making their way with haste to the trio. The Griffons were racing from their lairs, their roars of anger filling the air, warning all from the area. Even the babe Tambor had taken to wing, flying above his mother whose magick shielded her undefended belly now.

"Caise, Kai'el," she whispered her Consortors' names in fear as they rushed to her side.

"This cannot be," Garron growled, the black of his gaze flickering with a furious red. "That viperous bitch would not so dare to strike one I protect."

"Do something now," Marina cried out as her magick began to swirl around her and the lands themselves began to quake in fury at the challenge to its choice as Keeper Heir.

"At ease," they warned her quickly. "Your rage will only fuel the lands, Marina, and warn our enemies of our knowledge. Calm yourself. We go, love. Now."

Their magick surrounded her, and not for the first time, Marina found herself Shadow Walking, and terrified she wouldn't make it in time to save the Sorceress who knew not just how deep her loyalty truly did lie.

* * * * *

The Griffons were raging, their roars echoing outside the caverns as Sorceress magick and the darkness of all that was evil suddenly began to clash. Without thought, Astra sent her magick to close the cavern entrance to the beasts winging their way to the cavern, determined to protect her.

Alisante straightened from the cavern wall with a scream of rage, her eyes suddenly glowing black as blood-red magick poured from her fingertips toward the daughter she had never wanted, and had tried desperately to destroy in the womb.

With her, four Sentinel Warriors converged as well, the gray and red hues of their magick aligning with Alisante's and streaking far too quickly toward the Consortors Astra had given her heart and her soul to.

"No!" The cry tore from Astra's lips as she suddenly jumped between them and the fiery aura of a pure, blood-red evil magick streaking toward them.

As though time slowed as they tried to get to her, to push her back, Rhydan and Torran felt as though they were moving much too slow as they struggled to save the only link they possessed to life.

Before they could reach her a clash of magick sounded. The darkened rainbow of iridescent Veressi magick sliced between Astra and the reddened hues as the Guardians of the lands suddenly arrived in a hail of voracious power that sucked at the oxygen in the air.

At the same moment, Garron, Marina and the Sashtain Wizards were blocking the magick as well, protecting one too delicate, far too courageous Consortress as the bloody magick suddenly swung toward her.

The four Sentinel Warriors were blown back and, split from those of the darkness along with the Sorceresses, were suddenly thrown, hitting the cavern wall. Shaking their heads at the force of the blows, they were still able to send their magick, hues of gold, gray and amber, gentle blue and iridescent violets vied with fierce fiery brown to join the battle against the blood-red hues of evil and the blackened strands of a darkness straight from Shadow Hell as the four warriors who had attacked suddenly stood with a dragon nearly identical to Garron.

"Brother," the imposter growled in a voice that vibrated with evil. "So we meet again. Once more over Sorceresses whose value I greatly question."

"Question as you will," Garron snarled in a voice that thundered with rage. "Still will I protect them once again. And both we know how ended the battle we last fought." He smirked.

Steam emitted from the flared nostrils of the imposter. "Still yet, my power was greater, brother," the dragon reminded him. "'Twas the aid of our parents and siblings who have no concept of loyalty that won the battle for you."

Garron waved such a thought away as Astra watched the battle of words, her stomach tight with fear as she called out to the lands of her birth, to the Raging Seas that infused it and the magick that built beneath it to gather its power to greater force.

"And once again you have only piddling Sentinel Warriors to do your bidding, and reckless, greedy women without morals." Garron chuckled. "Have you learned nothing over the ages?"

Suddenly, blood-red magick shot toward Garron as a dragon's roar filled the cavern.

It was met with a rainbow of dark and light iridescent hues as Sorceresses, Sentinel Warriors, Astra's Keeper powers and Wizard Consorts alike threw their strength to Garron's and met the dark being with a power that seemed to grow, to intensify, to draw its breath from the soul of Sentmar's magick.

Thunder rolled as Astra threw her magick suddenly to her. Consortors combining with powerful Wizard magick, it strengthened, pierced the center of the veil of magicks to add even more strength to Garron's, the Veressi and the Sashtain Twins whose magick was infused with that of the Guardian of the Covenan lands. That magick, the greatest outside that of the One, met the evil drawn from the deepest reaches of Shadow Hell.

A scream of agony and rage pierced the cavern. In the blink of an eye, the dragon imposter disappeared and the traitorous warriors fell to the cavern floor as the Griffons were stopped outside the cavern by the spell Astra had quickly thrown at the opening to hold them from the danger of the evil inside.

Astra watched as their magick sizzled for but a second before the warriors were left to stare at the ceiling of the cavern in lifeless shock. Beside them, Alisante groaned, a whispered, "No, no, I cannot fail again. I cannot fail again," trembled from her lips.

She had attempted to destroy Astra even as she rested within the womb. How many other times before this had she attempted to murder the daughter who would have loved her?

The battle was over though. Finally, whatever dark force she had followed had been conquered, and all that was left would be to see to the former Keeper's punishment.

The land would never accept her again now. Should Alisante even attempt to step into the Mystic Forests after this, then the land itself would swallow her whole. The dark being who had tormented them since the arrival of the Wizard Twins had shown his presence and made himself known. There would be no peace now until somehow he was once again locked in the deepest pits where he could cause no harm. But Astra could sense there was much more at play here than simply a dark god's rage. There was more power backing this battle than history had claimed Dar'el could have.

Magick slowly receded, bringing the time of Astra's reckoning to hand as she faced the Ruling Wizards and the Guardian of the Covenan lands.

Turning to Marina, Astra went to one knee, head bowed.

"I submit to thee, Guardian," she whispered. "Punish me as you will."

She made no excuses. She begged for no mercy.

Instead, she faced what punishment would come for loving her Wizards and trusting in them above the proclamations of their guilt.

They were her heart, and she would make no excuses for it.

She was the Keeper of the Mystic Forests though, and she knew well the land had accepted her as such. No longer was she an heir. No longer would she be forced to wait to take the throne that was rightfully hers.

Her Guardian could not kill her.

She could not kill the Consorts Astra had taken to her heart.

But she could destroy the bonds of years of friendship and loyalty if she attempted in any way to punish the Wizards Astra loved.

There was no crime committed, and Astra would be damned before she would see her Wizards punished for that which they did not do.

Chapter Thirteen

ဆာ

No sooner had the words left her lips than Astra found herself not in the cavern where she had knelt before the Guardian of the Lands of Covenan, but rather instead inside a cavern beneath Sellane Castle.

The Crystal Palace, as it was called, dripped with crystals from the walls and ceiling. They were suspended as though they were multihued stars from the thinnest of webbed, crystallized spores of energy. They held sapphires, diamonds, emeralds, gems and precious stones. There were crystals of the finest ambers, amethysts and brilliant organza beads the color of a nearly opalescent orange, the softest, palest blue, violets and every color imagined.

Here, the power of any being, of any spell was multiplied. But there was also no access in or out of the cavern, and only a very, very select few knew it to be more than legend.

Even Astra had believed it to be legend before now.

Even here, Garron did not feel safe with whatever reason he had shadow jumped himself, Rhydan, Torran, herself, Marina and her Consorts the Sashtain Twins, and the Guardians of the Land of Cauldaran. Because within this magickal room of multihued starlight, he enclosed them within a shield of magick that twisted and swirled with all the colors of the rainbow. The colors of Garron's magick.

The shield was an impenetrable wall of magick that no others could see, hear or sense in any way. It was as though it simply did not exist to the eyes, ears, senses or magick of any being outside it. And only the greatest of magickal beings could do such a thing.

"Garron, what is the meaning of this magick?" Marina demanded as Astra watched the Veressi begin to weave their own magick through the wall of colors, their darkened hues nearly as powerful as those of the dragon's.

"Secrets will destroy not just this new Joining but will endanger any that come after it," Garron warned the Veressi as he ignored Marina's question. "I will not betray what you have given me, but I urge you, give what you can to ensure no harm befalls those I have taken beneath my protection."

His starlit black eyes watched the Wizards, their eyes as deep, as black as his own, their gazes just as intense as the dragon's as it seemed some message, some information passed between the three.

As the silent battle raged, Astra noticed the Guardian as she began probing at the shield with her magick. A frown marred her brow as she ran her hands over it, caressed it with the shades of her magick, infused with those of her Wizards.

As she did so, her lips tightened, her nostrils flaring, a sure indication of her rising anger.

"Dragon, you do not know what you ask," one of the Veressi breathed out roughly, the long fall of his silken hair brushing against his shoulders as he shook his head as though in weariness. "Our secrets are ones we were warned to hold—"

"So many secrets," Marina said then, moving from the shield to face the Veressi. "Within this shield Garron has created, there is more information than even you know. You made your mistake, Veressi, when you added to its strength."

Her Consorts now flanked her, arms crossed over their chests, their expressions disapproving and filled with ire as they now faced their former Guardians.

"How so, Guardian?" one asked gently. "This magick is free of any hint of individual strength or power. It is as water. Clear. Clean."

"And like water, that which comes from the oceans or the seas has a salty tang. From the mountain streams an icy bite, from the forest lakes a cool, refreshing sensation against the tongue. This magick," she gestured to the shield, "this magick is the same that I sensed when I entered my sister's room to find her as well as my mother having been taken. Tell me, dracas slime, where have you taken my queen mother and her heir?"

That was the familiarity she had sensed each time she had been in the presence of the Veressi.

Turning to them, she realized, just as the Sashtains had, her own Wizards now stood protectively at her side. What fearsome deeds had the Veressi done that her Wizards and Marina's would now guard them so closely?

The Veressi stared back at them, their expressions cleared, as though they were but carvings of some material to appear as living, breathing beings. In their eyes, there was no sign of warmth, nay, nor perhaps of life either.

The one who stood closest glanced behind him to the brother who leaned negligently against the wall.

Ruine, she was betting. Before as she had faced him, she had noticed his tendency to laze against the wall as though the effort of joining others was more than he could force himself to do.

"Sorceress, be careful what you accuse us of."

"I do not accuse, I asked a simple, straightforward question, Wizards. Where are my mother and my sister? For I know you have them, just as I now know each unique nuance of your magick. You could never hide it from me now, Wizards."

Anger surged through the confined space as the Guardian of Covenan, fueled by her fury and the strength of her Wizard Consorts, faced the Veressi.

"Guardian, be at ease." It was Garron who spoke, who attempted to still the suddenly lashing bands of furious, emerald magick beginning to whip about the Veressi. "The time now is for what can be given, not what can be demanded."

Marina turned on him, her face flushed, the red-gold of her hair seeming to fly about her as she faced the powerful beast.

"You have been our protector, Garron, yet you stand here before me and defend those who have stolen from us my mother and sister? Have your loyalties suddenly turned from those you have protected for a millennium to Wizards who all but drained us of life so many centuries ago?"

Powerful teeth snapped together in anger then as Garron suddenly stood to his full, impressive height.

"You throw out accusations as a child would," he smirked. "I had hoped the Joining with your Wizards would have matured you past such infantile behaviors. Was I wrong?"

Astra watched as Marina's shoulders stiffened and magick threatened to pour from her.

"Guardian, they are safe." Astra stepped forward quickly.

Pride was swirling with magick and creating a combination that could well destroy what had the potential to bring peace instead.

None had told her that she could not speak of what she had learned with her Joining with her own Consorts. Astra had been told to keep no secrets.

"And you know this how?" Marina turned on her furiously, her green eyes blazing with fear for her mother and sister.

Astra looked from Rhydan to Torran, saw the resignation in their expressions that matched the Veressis' and continued on.

None was urging her to hold her peace and the betrayal she had dealt her Guardian demanded some form of atonement. Some form of proof that it was not treason; rather it was love of men she knew had acted honorably.

"Through my Joining with the Delmari," she answered softly. "The danger of the dark one in Garron's form is growing and a select of Wizards have been chosen not just to aid in strengthening the rings of magick about the moons and within the magick lands, but also to protect those who are the most powerful." She looked to the Ruling Wizards. "Powerful Wizards willing to love the women who see them as monsters rather than men. The Kings of Cauldaran who took a princess Sorceress to Consort though she fought them at every turn."

She turned then to her Delmari. "And powerful Wizards who gave up what has been their birthright since Wizards first tasted magick, to come to this land and draw out those aiding the darkness. They did this, knowing it may mean perhaps losing their lands as well as the Consortress they have watched over since she was but a child. Rhydan and Torran did this because your Wizards refused to search for the Guardian to take as Consortress rather than the one their hearts cleaved to, unknowing she was one and the same.

"So my Consorts gave the illusion that they did this instead, Guardian. They gave the illusion of wishing to claim you, though they knew it could mean losing me. Because someone had to make the sacrifice to draw that darkness into the light."

Astra faced her Guardian, watched Marina's pain as it filled her eyes, and saw the tears that fell to her cheeks.

"I need to know Mother and Serena are safe," Marina whispered.

"Even if it means their deaths?" It was a Veressi who spoke. "Trust me when I say, Guardian, should your revered and most beautiful sister wish her freedom, then her freedom she would have. Should she see past her fears to the journeys she has taken over the past years, believing her travels to be only dreams, then she could return here to her home and return her mother to the throne. Until then, she is but a babe in the face of what could be coming on the horizon. Without the ability to tap into the power she holds, she is as weak as the Griffon babe when he was but stone, crushed beneath the cruelty of a Sorceress' hatred."

Marina stumbled back, all but falling into her Wizards' arms as she stared back at first Astra, then the Veressi.

"I would know if Serena held such power," she protested, seemingly shocked.

"And the dreams she shared with you when you were near broken from that attack as a fledgling Sorceress?" one asked gently. "The dreams of shadowed realms and adventures as warrioress?" He wiped his hand over his face as the other grimaced. "Sweet merciful Sentinels. Neither of you knew the danger you faced nor the danger you forced us to face when we joined you to protect the precious power the two of you possessed."

"And I am to know you are not playing some cruel, vicious trick such as your ancestors would have done?" Shock and disbelief filled her voice now. "I believed Guardians could not lie to another, but I doubt this sincerely now. How could you know of such things?"

Because they had taken those travels.

Astra remembered well the tales she and Serena told her and the others of the Sorceress Brigade when they were much younger. The adventures Serena wove as Marina slept to hold back the nightmares that would have come instead.

"Shall we introduce ourselves?" Raize asked mockingly. "I bid you adventure, Sorceress. I, Maxum, and my brother, Andrell, welcome you to the Vale of Sorcery. Which battle do you prefer?"

Hard lips quirked into simultaneous smiles of mockery.

"Tell me, Guardian," the other asked then. "Which did you prefer? That we leave her in her bed, her magick undefended as she drifted in the spell created by the god Dar'el? Or that we take her where his magick could not touch her, a place where she and her mother are protected even from the gods until she can protect herself?"

Astra, as the Guardian, could not hide her shock.

She was almost unaware of her movement to place herself closer to her Wizards, though she was not unaware of their arms, each crossing over her back, holding her securely lest that darkness steal her away.

Dar'el. The darkest of the darkness. The one Shadow Hell was created for. His punishment for bringing the cruelty of his parents, the Sentinel gods, upon his innocent brother's head and creating for Dal'el a life of misery.

The darkness that was evil had implanted its seed within the Sorceress goddess Musera at the time of her conception of Wizard Twins. Coming to her in a dream, he tied the life of his child to those of her Twins and laughed at her pain, mocked the purity and innocence of her love for her Twin gods and sought to destroy the bond created by their magick.

At the birth of the babes, each separate in looks, they had looked inside the babes and spoken to them, which that they be. And the child of darkness whispered to them. It was the child of darker skin, of darker eyes. One who could not hide his evil, they were told.

Only hours old and that child had known the darkness of deceit.

"He seeks to destroy the Sorceresses once again," Marina whispered, horrified.

The Veressi inclined their heads in agreement. "And Serena was gifted with the magick to return him to the pits for another millennium. But only if she survives, only if she willingly accepts her magick and her Consortors. Only, Keeper of Covenan, if she is strong enough to accept who she is and the fate given her."

Astra watched her Guardian's lips part, watched the fear that filled her eyes.

"Then we are doomed," she stated, her voice now hoarse and filled with horror. "We are doomed, Veressi, because there is nothing on this planet, even the darkness of that great evil, that my sister fears more than her own power."

"But, Guardian, there is nothing on this planet or beyond that she loves more than she loves her mother, her sisters and the Sorceresses who saved her at a time when that power would have destroyed her." Gentleness cloaked the two for but a moment before it was hidden once again. "And there is nothing she would not brave, even that power, as fearsome as it is, to save them."

And that, Astra knew, could well be all that would save them.

Chapter Fourteen

No decision had been made to her punishment. The Ruling Sashtain Wizards had commanded her Consortors to take her to her room. They were to remain with her, with only a spell of exit placed upon her door rather than actual guards.

That spell would not keep them bound inside; all it would do was notify the Guardian, her Consortors and Garron should they leave the rooms.

On the morn, they would discuss what would come next, the Keeper of Covenan informed her.

What would come next, Astra wondered. She could imagine nothing but banishment from the royal estates at the least. There was always the chance Marina could take from her the gifts Covenan had given her, her place as Keeper in Waiting of the Mystic Lands.

Only Marina herself had the power to do such a thing though, never a mother with such bleak, dark hatred inside her.

To take that power from her would be a fate worse than death, no matter who struck the magickal blow to sever the bonds.

To take her Wizards from her, though, would be death itself.

Marina had sent her to the magick pools beneath the castle rather than confining her with her Delmari Consortors. There, she was prepared for her warriors as she should have been that first night.

The curls that shielded the sensitive flesh of her pussy and aching clitoris were shorn by magick, leaving her forever bare to the forces of her Consortors' touch, as well as their magick.

She was cleansed thoroughly, Sorceresses in waiting as well as those older, Joined Sorceresses accompanied her, their talks of Joinings and men bringing gales of laughter to the much younger ladies attending Astra.

Would her Guardian have her put to death after ensuring her this night of magick and bonding with the Wizards meant to belong to Astra for life?

Surely she would not. Never had Astra known Marina to have a cruel bone in her body.

She was then taken to a solitary room with orders to rest from her trials. Exhaustion had been pulling at her for hours, but the thought that this might be her last night with her Consortors had kept her strength from waning.

Yet the moment her head touched the pillows and the brushed silk of the sheets drawn to her shoulders, Astra found herself sleeping, locked in dreams of happiness and her Consortors' smiles.

So much so that the twin moons of Sentmar were rising to herald the end of another day before she awoke to a meal and yet more of the gentle pampering reserved for Sorceresses heading for their Joining.

As the twin moons rose high in the night sky, she was taken to her room where her Consortors awaited her. Marina's message to her had been such that Rhydan and Torran had been behind closed doors with the Rulers in Waiting for most of the day, giving them much of the information they had gleaned from their attempts to discover how far the dark magick had infiltrated into the warrior sentinel ranks.

Now, after a day of rest without their touch, she found herself aching for them, her need for them settling in the pit of her stomach and clenching the depths of her pussy as she faced them.

"We have this night," Torran stated as he faced her, slowly disrobing by hand rather than magick. "We will not waste it with worry or doubt of our actions, Astra. This night, we will take as ours."

Her lips curved at the bit of amusement that statement brought.

"Did we not have the past day, before Alisante's less-than-polite intrusion, as our own?"

Rhydan gave a small grunt of acknowledgement. "Aye, and I am far from sated, Consortress. I would have far more of you."

With his words spoken, her clothing melted from her, disappearing and falling to the floor by the simple act of a wave of his hand.

They may have disrobed by hand, but it was by magick they removed her clothing, as though unable to wait to see her nakedness. The brush of air against the curves of her breasts, caressing the elongated tips of her nipples, had a small tremor of hunger racing down her spine.

Would she get enough of their touch?

Nay, she believed it would never be possible.

As she stood before them, their magick wrapped around her, she suddenly found herself impossibly aroused, more aroused than ever, by the fact that she was restrained.

Wizard magick bound her, its strength holding her in place. She was powerless, owning naught but her own magick in which to stroke or to pleasure them.

Breathing in slow and deep, determined to hold to the last thread of sanity, she sent that magick to do just that. To caress and stroke and pleasure them as she knew they would pleasure her.

It slipped along the tensed muscles of their legs, twined along their powerful thighs, then the sensation of her fingers wrapping about the hardened, thickened shafts had a gasp parting her lips.

Sensual magick telegraphed the feel of them, the heat and pulsating hunger in them to her fingertips, along her fingers and palms and had her aching for more.

"Ah Consortress, ease your magick before you steal the last of any control we may have," Torran groaned, his voice harsh now with his need.

Easing her magick along each hard length of their cocks, it then wrapped along the taut sacs of their balls, tightened delicately and stroked with movements as sensual as the hunger surging through her.

As they neared her, nothing mattered but feeling their touch. But touching them.

She didn't bother to fight the bonds of magick as they moved behind her.

"So long we have hungered for you, Consortress." Rhydan moved slowly behind her, his hands and his magick caressing down her back to her buttocks.

"We have ached for you, love," Torran rasped, his voice low, stroking like roughened velvet over her senses, weakening her with the need that rushed through her.

Behind her, Rhydan's hands stroked over her buttocks, his fingers gripping the rounded curves, parting them, sending a strike of sensual pleasure-pain at the tender opening.

Astra felt her breath tight in her chest as Rhydan lifted her then and carried her to the bed. Laying her to allow her stomach to rest against the bed, her warriors moved to the mattress with her.

"Ease up," Torran whispered, his magick lifting her shoulders as Rhydan's hands gripped her hips and raised her to her knees.

Kneeling before Torran, his hard warrior's fingers clenching his cock and pressing it to her mouth, Astra opened her lips willingly.

His other hand cupped her cheek as her lips opened over him and drew the hard crest inside. The immediate taste of male passion, a bit salty, all heat, seared her senses.

Behind her, Rhydan's lips touched the small of her back as his magick eased through the cleft of her rear and found the tender bud of her anus.

The threads of heated sensation had her back arching, a moan vibrating over the cock filling her mouth. This pleasure was insidious, thundering through her veins and igniting her magick with explosive results.

Closing her lips around the thick, flared crest of Torran's cock, she sucked it deep, her tongue lashing beneath, rubbing, tasting the throbbing excitement that filled it.

Rhydan kissed along her buttocks, parted her thighs farther and slid his hand between them. Cupping the bare mound of her pussy, his fingers found the saturated slit and swollen bud of her clit. Stroking there, rubbing against the side of the delicate bundle of nerves, he had her hips writhing before him.

Only to still, shock racing through her as Rhydan parted the rounded curves and slid his tongue to the tightly puckered entrance of her ass. It was shocking. Exciting. It was every sensual pleasure a woman could dream of.

His tongue licking and stroking, probing at the tiny entrance and pushing against it. Flares of reactive pleasure shot through her, heated her, and had her crying out against the heavy length of Torran's cock easing deeper between her lips.

"Sweet Sorceress," he groaned. "So hot your mouth is, wrapped around my cock. Suck it, love." His voice roughened as his hand slid into her hair, tightened and held her still as he began to fuck her mouth slow and deep.

The slow, inward strokes increased as she tightened her lips and sucked at the hard head. Her tongue rubbed beneath, causing his body to tighten further, his strokes gaining marginally in speed.

"How pretty," Torran moaned, his dark-blue gaze glittering with pleasure as he stared down at her. "How pretty your lips are stretched about my cock, your eyes gleaming with such magick."

His words stroked the sparkling explosions of magick running through her veins and intensified the pleasure of Rhydan's tongue probing at her ass.

"Suck my dick, love," Torran groaned, watching as Rhydan licked and probed at the sensitive entrance of her rear. "Show me how you enjoy Rhydan's touch. His tongue fucking your pretty ass."

Clenching, her body shuddering in pleasure, she could do nothing but cry out in protest as Torran pulled back, taking the treat she was enjoying with such relish as Rhydan's lips and tongue moved from her rear.

Then they were turning her, laying her back on the bed and trading places.

Torran came over her, his lips moving over hers, taking them, kissing her with a slow, sweet glide of his lips then turning the kiss decadently as his tongue came into play and his magick slid over her body. The caress of his power worked lower, brushing over her breasts, stroking to her stomach before sliding through the narrow slit of her pussy.

His lips traveled from her mouth to her neck. This tongue licked and stroked, moved to her nipples, covered a tight peak and suckled it into the heated warmth of his mouth.

As he played at the sensitive peaks his magick moved about the bare flesh of her pussy, stroking, slipping through the swollen, wet folds, preparing her flesh for his ultimate touch.

Abandoning her nipples Torran's kisses moved lower, his lips brushing over her stomach, moving to the aching flesh of her pussy as Astra turned to Rhydan, her hands reaching for him, her fingers curling over the length of his cock and drawing it to her as he knelt before her.

The engorged head of Rhydan's cock slipped past her lips as Torran's tongue slid through the slit of her pussy. Licking, stroking, probing at the shallow curves. As it circled her clitoris the tip rubbed against it, stroking the thin hood against the live bundle of nerve endings and sending her senses flying.

She was arching. Sucking at Rhydan's cock with abandon as Torran licked and sucked at her greedy pussy.

"Ah, sweet Astra," Rhydan moaned. "Show me how much you enjoy Torran's tongue lapping all that sweet cream from you pussy. Show me, love. Convince me how you need a hard, hot cock filling your little cunt as another tunnels up that tight, hot little ass."

She showed them. Nursing on his cock with abandon as her hips writhed beneath Torran's lips and tongue.

The air filled with magick. Strands of the palest blue, the richest of navy and the turbulent, darkening colors of emerald as it stroked over them.

The blues twined about her body, moved between the globes of her ass and the swollen folds of her pussy.

The navy wrapped about her nipples, stroked down her back, while the emerald color of her magick wrapped around their balls and Torran's cock, torturing them as they tortured her.

"I can take no more of this," Torran suddenly growled.

Rising from between her thighs as Rhydan drew back from her hungry lips, they lifted her, shifting her body until she was straddling Torran and Rhydan was moving swiftly behind her.

Positioning her, the broad head of his cock pressing into the folds of her pussy, Torran began sinking his cock into her sex. Slow, tortured thrusts. She took him an inch at a time as the feel of Rhydan's magick lubricating her ass had her bearing down on the cock fucking into her pussy.

She tried to writhe closer, her hips pressing down, desperate to fill her cunt with the wide, iron-hot heat of the shaft impaling her.

A harsh groan left Torran's lips as he suddenly thrust in hard, taking her to the hilt as Rhydan came closer behind her.

Hard hands held her hips still and steady, keeping her in place as the thick width of Rhydan's shaft pressed between her buttocks, tucked against the snug, puckered entrance of her ass and began to penetrate slowly.

Pleasure-pain, an agonizing splendor unlike anything imagined, attacked her senses then.

Astra could feel her anus milking his dick inside her, trying to pull him deeper as the feel of Torran's cock throbbing in her pussy nearly drove her to madness.

She couldn't move. Her hips were locked to Torran's, his magick and his hands holding her still, forcing her to experience each shallow thrust, each fiery, stretching thrust inside her ass as she cried out in an agony of need.

"Finish it," she cried out desperately, her nails raking at Torran's shoulders. "Mercy, Rhydan. Please, please fuck my ass now."

She screamed in pleasure. Or was it pain? Agony or ecstasy?

Whichever it was, the narrow channel took every inch of the turgid flesh and sucked at it, flexing around the pulsing shafts that filled her rear as well as her pussy.

Not that she was given but moments to adjust to the feel of them. To the pleasure attacking each portion of her body.

As though they, like her, could not bear the heightened sensations, they began thrusting inside her, hard, deep. Each hardened length of cock filled her, retreated, thrust inside her with brutally ecstatic strokes that had her crying out breathlessly.

She was locked within their arms, within their magick, and within a pleasure she wanted only to hold to her forever.

They fucked her in perfect rhythm, one impaling her as the other retreated, only to have the other return with a penetration that rocked her body as one pulled back.

Each thrust was filled with rapture, a loss of control and a need they were locked together within.

The primal intensity swirled inside them, binding them together with searing desperation.

Astra became lost in the haze of primitive hunger. Twin cocks filled her, harsh male groans filled the air and her flesh began to burn in response.

Each hard, thick impalement charged each crystalline spore of magick that thundered through her bloodstream. A whirlpool of sensations swirled violently through her, overtaking her, rocking through her.

Surviving such pleasure was not possible. Astra's cries became breathless, harsh as her muscles tightened on the thrusting cocks. Each stroke of their cocks fucking into her ignited another nerve ending, pushed the boundary and threw her closer to the edge. Each pulsing stroke filled her, stretched her, sent pleasure-pain tearing through her until it ignited her orgasm in such an explosion that she could only arch, a shattered attempt to scream leaving her throat. An attempt only. She could barely cry out. There was no breath left in her. There was nothing but the pleasure. Nothing but the incredible, agonizing ecstasy tearing through her as it tore through them.

Thick, pulsating jets of semen began to spurt inside her as each surged deep at once. Her orgasm burned higher, stronger. It shuddered through her, rocked her and sent her magick surging through flesh and bone straight to the souls of the Wizards possessing her.

Rhydan and Torran felt it. Felt her magick lock inside them, felt a pleasure that defied all known ideas of pleasure, release or ecstasy.

Even the Garden of Nirvana was not said to possess such powerful sensations. It tore through them, rocked their hips against her and flooded her further with their release.

It was more than they could have expected. More than they had ever dared to imagine. Pleasure surrounded and burned, blazed in rapture and overtook their senses.

And left them bonded with their Sorceress in ways they knew they could never imagine such a nightmare as to have it no longer exist.

As they collapsed beside her, Torran opened his eyes and stared back at his brother over their precious Consortress. Their greatest treasure. And silently, in a way that only Wizard Twins could, they made a vow.

No matter the consequences, they would lay down not just their lives but they would ensure the punishment of stealing this treasure's peace would be far greater than any could imagine.

She would not suffer her Joining with them.

They would ensure it.

Chapter Fifteen

ಐ

There were no Justices awaiting them when Astra and her Twins were shown into the throne room. There were no Wizard Justices, no guards.

There were only the Rulers in Waiting and the Guardian of the Powers of the Covenan Lands, along with the Cauldaran rulers and their Consortress, Brianna Sellane, the Veressi and the dragon Garron.

There was no accusation in their expressions, there was no sense of anger or recrimination.

As she neared the dais, she noticed the fourth, empty throne. Once, the three thrones would have held the queen and her daughters, Serena, Marina and Brianna.

Brianna's Joining with the rulers of Cauldaran exempted her from the ruling line, just as Marina's status of Guardian of Power exempted her. Serena's disappearance, as well as her mother's, left the ruling house near empty of a throne to guide it.

Marina's Joining with the Sashtain Wizards had for the first time placed Wizard Twins on the throne. Marina could not rule, but her Consort, or in this case, her Consorts could, until the queen or the heir returned. Or until another ruler could be selected in the case of their deaths.

Kneeling before the thrones, her Wizards went to one knee beside her.

Astra had exchanged the leathers of her warriors' attire for a brushed-silk gown of palest green and bordered by Gnomes lace in the color of the softest cream that Marina had bade one of the Sorceress of the Brigade to bring to her earlier.

On her feet she wore delicate shoes with soft leather soles sewn with brushed silk that matched the lace of her gown.

About her neck, dripping from her ears and placed strategically in her upswept curls were jewels gifted to her by the house of Sellane, and just before leaving their room, by the Wizards who now faced her sovereign in waiting beside her.

The jewels, glittering diamonds, rich emeralds and deep sapphires, sparkled with iridescence and life as her magick brought out the unique colors of each stone.

"Rise, Delmari," Caise Sashtain commanded.

Torran and Rhydan each allowed a hand to grip her upper arm and pull her up as well when she made no move to do so.

"You are Delmari as well, Sorceress," Kai'el informed her, his voice amused. "Sorceresses have been too long without their Wizards. You are Delmari now, just as they are Al'madere when the situation warrants it."

"Yes, sovereign," she answered softly.

Marina no longer sat on the throne between her two Consorts. She instead stood behind it, her fingers curled over the edge of the bright-blue brushed-velvet back.

"Sovereign, you know the reasons for our deceit," Torran stated. "What reason have we for being here?" He looked around the throne room, took in the absence of guards but the presence instead of the Verega, their Consortress and the Sashtain and Veressi Twins.

Caise Sashtain allowed his lips to quirk before turning to his Consortress.

"Queen Amoria declared there would be no Binding Ceremonies until Wizards were found to be either guilty or innocent of deceit against the throne," Marina said softly. "I have, as Consortress to the Sovereigns in Waiting, waved aside that command this one time for you, cousin, warrioress, and I give to you the Binding Ceremony I know you have always dreamed."

With a wave of her hand candles lit throughout the room, and Astra felt her breath catch in surprise and joy.

The magick of the sovereigns and the Guardian hiding the presence of those that now filled the throne room.

Friends and family, warriors and Wizards, and beneath an arch of magick stood the Wizard and Sorceress Priestesses who presided over the Bindings of those higher magickal sects.

"Marina?" She turned back to her cousin, uncertain now.

"Astra, you are guilty of no crime." Marina stepped from the throne dais and moved to her, taking both her hands in hers. "You committed no crime, instead, you have aided in bringing a great power to the land. One that will aid this upcoming battle in ways neither of us could have known. But, for your friendship, your loyalty and the years you have watched my back, Serena's and those of the Brigade, I give you this gift." She waved to the arch of magick. "Come, cousin, receive the blessing of the gods and know that you and yours now hold a place with the Select, as well as within our hearts."

Her Binding Ceremony.

As her Wizards moved, walking along the emerald-green tapestry that covered the floor, her heart swelled with joy, thankfulness and love.

This was the moment she had always dreamed of.

The moment of her Binding.

The first of many days with her Wizards, and the first day of a Joining that would complete them all.

Rhydan and Torran took their places before the Priests and Priestess who stood waiting to complete the ceremony.

Looking around, seeing no Wizard, no Sorcery to give her to her Wizards, she pushed back that lost, lonely child inside her that had always dreamed…

"Sorceress." It was Garron who spoke from behind her.

Turning, she watched the great dragon, his gaze filled with affection, with fondness. "Know you, that you are a favored one of the gods?"

Her lips parted in surprise as she glimpsed Camry moving to her.

Dressed in a pale-yellow-and-fiery-red dress that lovingly hugged her from breasts to hips, the Sorceress brought to her a trailing bouquet of white Fiera roses that glistened with the soft aura of diamond brilliance. The roses of the gods. It was said that only the goddess Musera possessed such roses and gifted them only to her most beloved Sorceresses.

"How..." she whispered as Camry kissed her cheek gently.

"They were delivered by a Thunderbird," the Sorceress whispered in awe. "How lovely are they?"

They were incredible. There were dozens upon dozens of the pure-white-diamond glistening flowers, trailing from where she held them to her knees.

"The gods have bequeathed to you a dream, Sorceress," Garron stated, his voice rasping and low. "Turn child, and see what they have sent you."

A gasp filled the room as she turned—slowly she turned and faced the impossible. A dream she had been certain—had known could never be hers.

Yet he stood before her.

Dressed in the white uniform of brushed silk, the colors of the house of Al'madere adorning his broad shoulders. His thick, dark-blond hair was secured at his nape, his golden gaze filled with love and pride as his bronzed flesh radiated with life.

"Do you accept your Wizards with love, joy and with a willing spirit?" her father asked her, his deep voice, never forgotten, always loved, wrapping around her as tears filled her eyes and joy swelled her heart.

"Papa," she whispered, reaching out to touch him, feeling the warmth of his face, the rasp of the closely trimmed beard he had always worn.

So handsome he was, with that look of having aged that he would have possessed had he lived.

"My treasured child." Reaching up, he cupped her cheek with the utmost gentleness, his palm warm, the callouses his palm possessed rasping at her cheek. "Do you accept your Wizard Twins willingly?" he asked again.

"With all my heart." She was crying, but they were sobs of such joy. "How is this possible? How are you here?"

"A gift from Musera, given by the One, pleaded for by your Wizards, precious, for your strength, your acceptance and your gentle heart in the face of Alisante's treachery." The gentleness of his voice was a memory that had sustained her as a child and now wrapped around her in truth. "Your Wizards have loved you from afar, protected you and sought to comfort you. And now they have lent their magick and a vow to the One to always cleave to you and yours, in exchange for this gift. But know this, they would have given you that and more, whether the One heeded their pleas or not."

His gaze shadowed as he spoke of Alisante, then cleared as he tucked a strand of hair, the color so similar to his own, from her shoulder to trail behind her back.

"I always watch over you, daughter," he whispered then, for her ears alone. "Always I have been close, lending to Musera and your Wizards my voice in awakening the One. Giving to him the truth of the purity of your love, the strength of your dedication, your joy and your acceptance of the land and the magick that are so much a part of you. I will always be close."

He took her hand then, placed it on his arm and turned her to the Wizards who awaited her.

She could not take her eyes from him.

Her precious papa.

This had been her dream of her Binding Ceremony. To have her papa, so brave and strong, lead her to the Wizards she would share her life and her lands with.

Leading her past friends, family, her sisters in battle, her Guardian Keeper and those who had been a part of her life for so long, she could think of nothing that could be more perfect than this gift.

As they neared the altar of the One and the Select, her Wizards stepped to the center of the aisle, turned to her, watching her with such love that their magick was an aura around them in such differing shades of blue that they glowed.

Stopping before them, her papa lifted her hand to them and asked, "Do ye Wizards Delmari accept my beloved daughter and open your Wizards' souls to all that she is?"

"Sorcerer Al'madere, so we do," Rhydan answered, his voice echoing with his vow.

"Sorcerer Al'madere, so we do," Torran repeated, his own voice throbbing with the truth of his vow.

"So then do I give to you this precious daughter. Know ye that I always watch over her. And know ye that in this treasure you are given beats a heart that the One created to cleave unto you, to remain open, willing and filled with the purity of a Sorceress' magick and a woman's pure, enduring love."

"So do we accept, Sorcerer Al'madere," her Wizards swore. "We open our souls to hers, our heart to hers. We give to her our strength, and forever more, we give to her our magick."

That magick glowed, built, then as she watched in awe it flowed from them, merged with hers then as she watched, the merging colors flowed around them, around her, enclosing them in a lush, heated aura of such magick it stole her breath as it seemed to disappear into the pores of her Wizards even as she felt it sinking into hers.

"Come ye to the gods, Torran, Astra and Rhydan," the Sorceress Priestess said gently, her voice trembling with the same wonder Astra felt weaving through her as her papa moved to where her Wizards had stood as she walked to them. "Come ye, to the heart of each—"

To the heart of each.

To her Twins, and her Twins to her.

Together, as the gods had meant them to be.

Epilogue

ဢ

The magick room made by the "shield" they had created enclosed the most precious of treasures that had been gifted to Sentmar.

It contained not just a princess but a Sorceress Sentinel of Power, a being unheard of for over two millennia. A Sorceress with the ability to command, control and oversee the magick of all the lands, not just those of one, but of all Sentmar.

Fair of face, delicate of body.

Lips that held the sweetest pout, and eyes the color of the deepest of green seas.

Slender legs and rounded thighs, hips a man could grip as he pressed into her, possessed her.

A lithe and desirous body that he and Ruine knew they would be able to hold back from not much longer.

She was beauty in its ultimate form.

She was magick in its deepest purity.

She was the salvation of a land slowly being overrun by dark magick and had no idea the abilities she held within her small body.

"What do we do from here?" Raize asked, his tone a dark, fearsome growl.

Ruine sighed at the question and shook his head. "At this moment, brother, I am not certain. Like the Pixie the Claemai bound to them, we cannot force either her heart nor her touch. Though I feel it would not matter. Her hatred already runs deep for us."

"Aye, this is true," he agreed. "It is but a hatred she will soon forget, brother. Once she touches the magick within herself and opens those doors, then her time here within this shield will be forgotten."

"Should she do so." Raize highly doubted she would. "Our time is nearly at an end. Still, I do not feel her in the Shadow Planes, nor do I sense her magick outside the room we created for her."

And they could push her no further.

They could not touch her.

They could not claim her.

She was created for them alone, their natural Consortress, her power stronger, more deeply in touch with the center of magick that flowed through the land, yet she refused to access it.

It presented more of a problem then they wished to contemplate.

"To release her would be the same as placing a babe before a Harpie," Raize growled with an edge of impatience. "The darkness moving into Covenan would devour her."

"We may have to alter our plans then," Ruine suggested. "Does she not step into the Shadow Planes, then she will be doomed."

They stared back at her as she slept, innocence, dreamless sleep, and despaired of ever finding a way to force her into her own escape.

* * * * *

"She will be doomed—" Serena caught the last of the conversation as she slipped past the shield that held her physical body bound and sent her magick reaching out through the caverns where she was being held.

The castle was huge. She had used her time in the prison she was locked within to scout it as thoroughly as possible, but had only recently found her mother.

As she had been each time Serena materialized in her magick form into her room, Queen Amoria was pacing the floors.

She jumped at the sight of the wavering magick that revealed her daughter's presence, but it was love and thanksgiving that filled her expression and her eyes.

"Have you contacted Garron yet?" Amoria questioned her, the anger still yet throbbing in her tone. "He could get us from this place, Serena."

She could get them from there. She was no fledgling, she clearly remembered the Shadow Planes and how to use them, just as she remembered the dangers that lived within them. Dangers she feared she and her mother might not survive because the protectors who once lingered there had not been present for many cycles.

"I cannot find a way to send the form of my magick from the castle, Mother," Serena revealed. "I have tried, but this place where we are being held is too well protected."

"And who holds us? The Sentinels have mercy on them once Garron learns of this. He will not stand for such betrayal." Hands clenched to fists at her side, her mother swung away from her, anger throbbing in her voice with each word.

And how Garron must worry for the queen he had given his heart to, Serena thought silently, refusing to voice the thought to her mother.

She had known for ages exactly who Garron was, and the deceit he had practiced upon the house of Sellane as well. Unfortunately, that deceit had been no treason nor criminal act. Though she feared her mother would not see it quite that way.

"I hope to perhaps connect with another being this night," Serena revealed. "There is a Pixie within distance of my magick, I believe. I can sense her clearly, but I have not yet identified her. She would send word to Garron."

"Yes." Amoria shook her head as she raked her fingers through her still-vibrant, red-gold hair. "The Pixies have always given us their loyalty."

She turned back to her daughter, staring at the wavering form of magic as Serena stood calm and composed before her.

There were no emotions seeping out to color the vibrant green hues of magick that made up her form. As though emotion had been vanquished long ago, she had often thought.

Sweet mercy, what had happened to her child that she no longer felt those great surges of laughter and joy?

What a failure she had been as a mother, Amoria castigated herself. Brianna had feared Wizard magick to the point that she was convinced it would be rape. Sweet Marina had been all but raped, and had feared telling her mother. And Serena, her heir, the child she had groomed to sit upon the throne of Covenan, had apparently found a way to tame all the emotion that had once existed around her.

"Are you well, Mother?" Serena asked in concern as Amoria continued to stare back at her in confusion.

Her mother nodded, but it was a halfhearted gesture at best. "Aye, child, I'm fine. Fine," she was assured before Amoria asked, "Serena, why did you never tell me you could travel with your magick in such a way?"

Serena clasped her hands before her. "Perhaps I wasn't aware I could, Mother."

Amoria said nothing more. Her daughter would not reveal the truth to her when she stated a denial in such a way. Nay, not a denial, a deception. It was a lie veiled within a half truth. She knew well, she had used such things herself.

She battled the tears and the fear she felt for the gentle young woman she had always felt had been most like her. "I love you, Serena."

Confusion flickered through her daughter's gaze then. "As I love you, Mother. I should know about the Pixie soon."

185

Just as quickly, her daughter was gone.

Amoria lifted her fingers to her lips, fighting to hold back her tears when another form materialized.

This one was of flesh and blood, leathery scales and a gaze filled with somber sympathy.

"What happened to her, Garron?" She didn't turn to the dragon.

She felt him, knew he was there. This was no imposter. She had known this dragon her entire life, and knew the feel of him as she knew nothing else.

"She has many fears," he said softly. "And she's had many adventures within the Planes, my Queen. She knows the dangers there now, and she greatly fears them."

"Does she sense my knowledge of all this?" She waved her hand at her prison before turning to the dragon.

His large head shook slowly. "But I cannot stay long, for she will sense me."

"Have the Veressi move me." Her head lifted, determination filling her. "Have them take me to the Shadow Planes. She will come for me there."

His brow lifted. "You who abhor the Planes?" he questioned her. "Are you certain, my Queen, this is what you wish?"

She nodded slowly. "She is my daughter, Garron. She and her sisters are all I have left of their father, of the heart I lost so very long ago. I will do what I must."

"Even face your own fears?"

She nodded slowly. "That is a very small price to pay for my daughters' safety. A very small price indeed."

Men of August 4: August Heat
Sealed with a Wish
Soul Deep
The One
Wizard Twins 1: Ménage a Magick
Wizard Twins 2: When Wizards Rule
Wizard Twins 3: Twin Passions
Wolf Breeds 1: Wolfe's Hope
Wolf Breeds 2: Jacob's Faith
Wolf Breeds 3: Aiden's Charity
Wolf Breeds 4: Elizabeth's Wolf

Print Books:
A Wish, A Kiss, A Dream
B.O.B.'s Fall *(with Veronica Chadwick)*
Bound Hearts 2 & 3: Submission Seduction
Bound Hearts 4 & 5: Wicked Sacrifice
Bound Hearts 6 & 7: Shameless Embraces
Broken Wings
Cops and Cowboys *(anthology)*
Ellora's Cavemen: Tales from the Temple I *(anthology)*
Feline Breeds 1: Tempting the Beast
Feline Breeds 2: The Man Within
Feline Breeds 3: Kiss of Heat
Legacies: Dragon Prime
Legacies 1: Shattered Legacy
Legacies 2: Shadowed Legacy
Legacies 3: Savage Legacy
Manaconda *(anthology)*
Men of August 1: Marly's Choice

About Lora Leigh

ᘓᘔ

Lora Leigh lives in the rolling hills of Kentucky, and is often found absorbing the ambience of this peaceful setting. She dreams in bright, vivid images of the characters intent on taking over her writing life, and fights a constant battle to put them on the hard drive of her computer before they can disappear as fast as they appeared. Lora's family, and her writing life co-exist, if not in harmony, in relative peace with each other. Surrounded by a menagerie of pets, friends, and a teenage son who keeps her quick wit engaged, Lora's life is filled with joys, aided by her fans whose hearts remind her daily why she writes.

ᘓᘔ

The author welcomes comments from readers. You can find her website and email address on her author bio page at www.ellorascave.com.

Tell Us What You Think

We appreciate hearing reader opinions about our books. You can email us at Service@ellorascave.com (when contacting Customer Service, be sure to state the book title and author).

Why an electronic book?

We live in the Information Age—an exciting time in the history of human civilization, in which technology rules supreme and continues to progress in leaps and bounds every minute of every day. For a multitude of reasons, more and more avid literary fans are opting to purchase e-books instead of paper books. The question from those not yet initiated into the world of electronic reading is simply: *Why?*

1. *Price.* An electronic title at Ellora's Cave Publishing runs anywhere from 40% to 75% less than the cover price of the exact same title in paperback format. Why? Basic mathematics and cost. It is less expensive to publish an e-book (no paper and printing, no warehousing and shipping) than it is to publish a paperback, so the savings are passed along to the consumer.

2. *Space.* Running out of room in your house for your books? That is one worry you will never have with electronic books. For a low one-time cost, you can purchase a handheld device specifically designed for e-reading. Many e-readers have large, convenient screens for viewing. Better yet, hundreds of titles can be stored within your new library—on a single microchip. There are a variety of e-readers from different manufacturers. You can also read e-books on your PC or laptop computer. (Please note that Ellora's Cave does not endorse any specific brands.

You can check our website at www.elloraascave.com for information we make available to new consumers.)

3. *Mobility.* Because your new e-library consists of only a microchip within a small, easily transportable e-reader, your entire cache of books can be taken with you wherever you go.

4. *Personal Viewing Preferences.* Are the words you are currently reading too small? Too large? Too... ANNOYING? Paperback books cannot be modified according to personal preferences, but e-books can.

5. *Instant Gratification.* Is it the middle of the night and all the bookstores near you are closed? Are you tired of waiting days, sometimes weeks, for bookstores to ship the novels you bought? Ellora's Cave Publishing sells instantaneous downloads twenty-four hours a day, seven days a week, every day of the year. Our webstore is never closed. Our e-book delivery system is 100% automated, meaning your order is filled as soon as you pay for it.

Those are a few of the top reasons why electronic books are replacing paperbacks for many avid readers.

As always, Ellora's Cave welcomes your questions and comments. We invite you to email us at Service@elloraascave.com or write to us directly at Ellora's Cave Publishing Inc., 1056 Home Avenue, Akron, OH 44310-3502.

MAKE EACH DAY MORE *EXCITING* WITH OUR

ELLORA'S CAVEMEN

CALENDAR

☥ WWW.ELLORASCAVE.COM ☥

ELLORA'S CAVE
Romanticon

Annual convention
for women who
refuse to behave

CPSIA information can be obtained at www.ICGtesting.com
Printed in the USA
LVOW05s1655230714

395663LV00001B/104/P

9 781419 967740